本书出版受到教育部中外语言交流合作中心 2021 年度国际中文教育创新项目 "'诗译成都,语话天府'国际中文课程暨'成都最美古诗词 100 首'双语文化系列读本"(项目编号:21YH012CX5)资助,特此致谢!

编委会成员

主编◎杜　洁　【美】王亦歌

副主编◎王利华　杨　茜　林　莺　田海稣

诗歌翻译◎王亦歌

诗歌赏析编译◎王利华　杨　茜　周怡乔　杨　蓓　熊亭玉

　　　　　　陈　欣　牛晓丹　朱　玲　郭粒粒　刘　颖

书法艺术◎田旭中

绘画设计◎田海稣

英文编辑◎【美】瑚雨然

赏析审校◎蔡　宁

Editors ◎ Du Jie　Wang Yige

Associate Editors ◎ Wang Lihua　Yang Xi　Lin Ying　Tian Haisu

Poem Translator ◎ Wang Yige

Poem Appreciation Translators ◎ Wang Lihua　Yang Xi　Zhou Yiqiao　Yang Bei

　　　　　　　　　　　　　　　Xiong Tingyu　Chen Xin　Niu Xiaodan　Zhu Ling

　　　　　　　　　　　　　　　Guo Lili　Liu Ying

Calligraphy Art ◎ Tian Xuzhong

Art Design ◎ Tian Haisu

English Editing ◎ Lorraine Hu

Poem Appreciation Proofreading ◎ Cai Ning

本书为成都大学2021—2023年人才培养质量和教学改革立项项目
"诗译成都，语话天府——成都最美古诗词国际中文在线课程
暨双语读本体系构建与实践"（项目编号：cdjgb2022039）成果，
并获成都市2022年教育国际交流合作奖补专项资金项目支持。

诗译成都　语话天府

成都最美百首古诗词中英双语鉴赏　卷二

One Hundred of the Most Beautiful Poems of Chengdu: Land of Poetry and Abundance　Volume 2

主编◎杜　洁　【美】王亦歌

编译◎成都大学海外教育学院

四川大学出版社
SICHUAN UNIVERSITY PRESS

图书在版编目（CIP）数据

诗译成都 语话天府 ：成都最美百首古诗词中英双语
鉴赏．卷二：汉英／杜洁，（美）王亦歌主编；成都大
学海外教育学院编译．— 成都：四川大学出版社，
2022.12

ISBN 978-7-5690-5894-9

Ⅰ．①诗… Ⅱ．①杜… ②王… ③成… Ⅲ．①古典诗
歌—鉴赏—中国—汉、英 Ⅳ．① I207.2

中国国家版本馆 CIP 数据核字（2023）第 064059 号

书　　名：诗译成都　语话天府——成都最美百首古诗词中英双语鉴赏　卷二
　　　　　Shiyi Chengdu Yuhua Tianfu—Chengdu Zuimei Bai Shou Gushici Zhong-ying Shuangyu Jianshang Juan Er
主　　编：杜　洁　[美]王亦歌
编　　译：成都大学海外教育学院

丛书策划：周　洁
选题策划：周　洁
责任编辑：周　洁
责任校对：余　芳
装帧设计：田海稣
责任印制：王　炜

出版发行：四川大学出版社有限责任公司
　　　　　地址：成都市一环路南一段 24 号（610065）
　　　　　电话：（028）85408311（发行部）、85400276（总编室）
　　　　　电子邮箱：scupress@vip.163.com
　　　　　网址：https://press.scu.edu.cn
印前制作：成都墨之创文化传播有限公司
印刷装订：四川盛图彩色印刷有限公司

成品尺寸：185 mm×230 mm
印　　张：8.5
字　　数：183 千字

版　　次：2023 年 4 月 第 1 版
印　　次：2023 年 4 月 第 1 次印刷
定　　价：88.00 元

扫码获取数字资源

四川大学出版社
微信公众号

FOREWORD

My first impressions of Chengdu, in 2017, still resonate, specifically as strong sensory perceptions: first through the biting spices of Sichuan's signature hotpot, strikingly scarlet from its use of an enormous amount of chili peppers. Exhausted and hungry after a 24-hour journey from our home in Durham, New Hampshire, through Shanghai and finally to Chengdu, my daughter, Ellie, and I, upon landing, were treated to Chengdu's signature peppery hotpot dish. While adjusted slightly for non-locals in the restaurant's kitchen, meaning the dish's bite was slightly subdued, each piquant spoonful rounded off the corners of my jetlag. The fog of travel lifted for an hour or so, before I collapsed into bed, the taste of Chengdu lingering on my tongue. Post-jetlag and eyes wide open, I awoke the next morning to discover Chengdu's vibrant visual images of nature, architecture, and living history.

Four years later, in the winter of 2021, I am working with Wang Yige, this project's translator, and Ellie as proofreader of the selected poems for this volume. So immersed in the poetic sights, sounds, emotions, and tastes of what was once called the Brocade City, I am once again transported in memory to the treasures of this city, when I lectured at Chengdu University. After that hot pot introduction to Chengdu cuisine, I continued to eat my way through the city, sometimes dining in elegant restaurants on twelve-course meals, other times queuing at the faculty canteen（at only five yuan a meal）, or standing, slurping noodles or chopsticking dumplings, at the campus's back gate, where snack carts hawked a dizzying variety of cheap choices to hungry students.

Several poems speak of Chengdu Plain's famous Dujiangyan irrigation system. Built over two thousand years ago and still in use today, it stands as an engineering miracle and a UNESCO World Heritage Site. While assisting Yige in choosing language and logical order for each poem, the verses took me back to the walking path around the irrigation system that borders the Min River: water ringed by swaying grasses; pine trees behind whose boughs sat colorful shrines of red and gold or, sometimes, rough wooden structures of elegant simplicity; and open spaces whose faces lay upturned to the blue sky. The hike concluded at a small collection of shops and restaurants, where we hungrily consumed handmade wheat noodles, prepared on sight, drenched in spicy sauce and sesame seeds. Chengdu's sights and flavors remain intertwined.

On another day, we were driven through the city's inner ring road, lined by evenly planted palm trees, to Jinli Street, a stone-paved walkway decorated with red lanterns, preserving its two-thousand-year-old architectural ancestry. After passing through a stone gate entryway, shops, housed in wooden buildings, beckoned to residents and tourists alike to enter their wide open store fronts. Inside, a riot of colors and objects greeted us: silk scarves, embroidered garments, fans, lamps, stationery, leather goods, t-shirts, and toys. Purveyors of traditional Sichuan snacks fried, rolled, and tossed their treats at small carts, attracting attention as they offered sticks of spun sugar or paper cones of peanut-covered candy. While the alley's pace is one of leisure, when the crowds and heat weigh on the weary shopper, duck into a teahouse—perhaps a Starbucks, but no guarantee that this popular place, even

in China, will provide quiet sanctuary—a restaurant, or stay overnight in one of Jinli's many hotels whose windows face the lively shopping alley.

Indeed, one often finds relief in this densely populated city, intensely hot and humid in the summer, at the edges of a pond, arched with wooden bridges. The center of Chengdu University housed such a tranquil spot, serving as a respite, a point of beauty, and for me, a visual campus marker by which to navigate my whereabouts when on early morning jogs.

For a walk through wooded paths and bamboo groves that promise the sight of a variety of pandas, not only storybook's black and white "cats," as the animals are translated from Chinese, I remember fondly an excursion to the Chengdu Panda Base. A research center for giant pandas, it invites visitors to enjoy the usually rare view of pandas, here a common sight as they lolled on wooden structures built for their daily respite, chewed methodically on bamboo, slow as sloths in the summer heat. The sight of so many black and white bodies in a huge habitat built to the specifications and needs of this animal, prompted me to ask myself, where are a myriad of poems about these curious, gentle creatures?

That Chengdu was once called the Brocade City, because of its famed embroidery, struck me as apt for a metropolis that weaves together nature, history, and technology, including the world's largest single building if assessed by floor space—the New Century Global Center. It houses not only shops and restaurants, but a water park equipped with a wave pool. On one of the Center's upper levels, a series of glass flooring blocks allow brave pedestrians to stroll across their transparent faces, as if precariously walking on air.

My experiences in Chengdu, too, were like walking on air, brought back so vividly during this poetry project. Colorful like embroidery, serene by turns, the poems in this collection memorialize, for me, the city, its past, traditions, history, and its people. I hope this publication's celebratory intent will encourage others to follow in my footsteps, but more importantly, in those of the famous poets whose work will transport you, through all of your senses, to Chengdu, the Brocade City, nestled in the southwest province of Sichuan.

Dr. Monica Chiu
Professor of English
University of New Hampshire, U.S.A.
May 20, 2022

序言

我对成都的第一印象是在 2017 年，至今仍挥之不去，尤其是强烈的感官感受：首先是四川特色火锅辛辣的香料，大量的红辣椒，鲜红得惊人。我和女儿埃莉（Ellie）从新罕布什尔州达勒姆（Durham）的家出发，经过上海，到达成都，24 小时的旅途之后我们精疲力竭，饥肠辘辘。飞机落地后，迎接我们的是成都招牌辣味火锅。为了适应外地人的口味，饭馆的厨师给我们调整了辣味，上的是微辣。但每一口中的调味品都刺激着我的神经，减轻了我的时差反应。大约有一小时，我借此暂时忘却了旅途的疲惫，然后就彻底瘫倒在床了，成都的味道却依然在舌尖徘徊。倒完时差的第二天早上，我睁大眼睛，呈现在我眼前的是充满活力的成都——它的环境、建筑和鲜活的历史。

四年后，2021 年冬天，我和本项目的翻译王亦歌再次合作，埃莉也成为这本诗选的校对。这座被称为"锦城"的城市那充满诗意的景象、声音、触觉、情感和味道围绕着我，我再一次陷入那些珍贵的回忆之中。我曾在位于这座城市的成都大学讲学。可以说我是一路吃过来的：有时在菜品齐全的高档餐厅，有时在一顿饭只需 5 元的教师食堂，甚至在学校后门跟饥肠辘辘的学生们一起站在路边摊旁呲溜呲溜地吃面条，或者尝试用筷子挑着饺子吃。学校后门有一排排小吃车摊点，车上摆着令人眼花缭乱的各式实惠食物，吸引着食欲正盛的学生们。

成都平原著名的都江堰灌溉系统也在几首诗中被提及。这是建于两千多年前至今仍在运行的一个工程奇迹，被列入联合国教科文组织世界遗产名录。在我们为每首诗的翻译推敲措辞的过程中，这些诗句又把我带回了岷江边都江堰旁的那条小路：水面被摇曳的水草环绕；透过松树的树枝，隐约可见色彩斑斓的寺庙，红色的、金色的，偶尔也会有古朴典雅的木结构建筑；以及一处处仰视着蓝天的开阔地带。走累了，我们就在商店和餐馆林立的地带停下，狼吞虎咽地吃上一碗手工面。这是一种浇上辣酱、撒上芝麻、立等可取的面条。成都的景色和味道在心头萦绕。

有一天，我们乘车沿着一环路到了锦里。一环路是一条两旁种满棕榈树的环线，而锦里则是一条石砌的步行街，两旁挂满了红灯笼，传承着它两千年历史的建筑血统。穿过入口的石门，街两边是木制建筑内的商店，个个店门敞开欢迎人们光顾。店里商品琳琅满目，令人目不暇接：丝绸围巾、刺绣服装、扇子、灯具、文具、皮具、T恤和玩具。小商贩的小推车上摆着各种传统四川小吃，有炸的、有卷的、有拌的。车上的棉花糖、纸筒花生糖刺激着人们的味蕾。虽然这条小巷的步调是休闲的，但当那些疲惫的顾客在拥挤和高温的驱使下躲进茶馆——也可能星巴克时，不能确保这个即使在茶的国度也深受大众喜爱的地方能给大家提供一个安静的庇护所。包括饭店，或者在锦里那些窗户朝向热闹的购物街的酒店住上一夜，都是如此。

事实上，在这个人口稠密、夏季潮热的城市，一个有独木拱桥的池塘就可以给人们带来慰藉。成都大学校内就有这样一个安静的地方。它既是一个休憩地，又是一个风景秀丽的景点。对我来说，它还是一个独特的校园地标，清晨慢跑时它可以给我指引方向。

我清楚地记得去成都熊猫基地的一次旅行。漫步在枝叶茂密的竹林中，你可以看到各种各样的熊猫，不只是故事书中讲的那种黑白相间的"猫"，就像它在中文里的意思。这里作为一个大熊猫研究中心，它吸引游客前来参观罕见的大熊猫日常生活的景象。在这里，你可以看到它们或者懒洋洋地躺在木架子上休息，或者慢悠悠地嚼竹子，就像夏天的树懒一样。身处专门按照这些黑白相间的大块头的体型和需求而建造的大型栖息场所，我不禁在想，那些关于这些奇特而温顺的动物的诗在哪里？

成都曾因其著名的刺绣而被称为"锦城"，这让我感觉它是一个将自然、历史和科技融合在一起的大都市。这里有以建筑面积来衡量的世界最大单体建筑——新世纪环球中心。里面不仅有商店和餐馆，还有一个带人工造浪池的水上公园。在中心的高层有一条玻璃栈道，勇敢的行人可以在这条透明栈道上行走，仿佛险象环生的空中漫步。

本诗歌项目又把我带回了成都，往事历历在目，像空中漫步一样浮现脑际。时而斑斓如锦绣，时而宁静如大海。让我想起这座城市，它的过去、它的传统、它的历史和它的人民。希望这套书的出版能够鼓励更多的人跟随我的脚步，更重要的是，跟随那些著名诗人的脚步。他们的作品能把你的感知带到成都，带到这座位于中国西南地区的四川省的锦城。

莫妮卡·邱博士
美国新宾夕法尼亚大学英语系教授
2022 年 5 月 20 日

编者
的话

在教育部中外语言交流合作中心和成都大学的大力支持下，成都大学海外教育学院组建了一个由多位专家参与的团队，编译"诗译成都　语话天府"丛书。丛书共包括100首诗歌，分四册陆续出版，以飨读者。

成都平原被誉为天府之国，物产丰饶，气候温润，多民族在此和谐共处，是华夏文明的主要起源地之一。大诗人李白就对成都平原的富饶美丽不吝赞美之词，在其《上皇西巡南京歌十首·其二》中夸赞道："九天开出一成都，万户千门入画图。草树云山如锦绣，秦川得及此间无。"

近年来，三星堆出土的诸多文物更是举世惊艳，显示成都平原在远古时代就有了极其精美的青铜器和玉器，其后又有瑰丽多彩的蜀锦、蜀扇等传统工艺品。这在古诗词中可窥见一斑，如描绘蜀锦的"蜀纻于今夸丽密，浪花堆里缬芙蓉"，描写蜀扇的"出匣风初转，垂纶半月圆。人间遗玉柄，犹是汉宫年"等。

成都的富饶离不开岷江雪水的润泽，可以说，两千多年前举世无双的都江堰工程直接奠定了天府之国的基础。所谓"一自金堤凿，三都水则分。……万户饶粳稻，千秋荐苾芬"，清澈的岷山雪水从此源源不断地流入这片广袤的平原，既灌溉了作物，也催生了诸多行业和文化：如文人墨客心心念念的"薛涛诗思饶春色，十样鸾笺五采夸"中的薛涛笺，如"峨峨雪色涉苍龙，直上汶江锦万重"及"女郎剪下鸳鸯锦，将向中流匹晚霞"

中的华丽蜀锦，如"锦里多佳人，当垆自沽酒"及"卓女家临锦江滨，酒旗斜挂树头新。当垆不独烧春美，便汲寒浆也醉人"中的酒肆文化，以及"麻婆陈氏尚传名，豆腐烘来味最精。万福桥边帘影动，合沽春酒醉先生"中的成都特色饮食文化……这些都是来自雪山的馈赠，汩汩清源流进成都平原，又奔向锦江、青衣江、浣花溪等数不清的支流，绘就了绵延不绝的诗意成都。

"曾城填华屋，季冬树木苍。喧然名都会，吹箫间笙簧"，这是杜甫从天水逃难到成都后对成都的第一印象。成都的繁华秀美深深打动了杜甫，诗人在浣花溪边安置下来，开始了安定惬意的四年时光。也正是因为杜甫，闻名遐迩的诗句成了天府诗歌文化一个不可或缺的部分，如"晓看红湿处，花重锦官城""细雨鱼儿出，微风燕子斜""两个黄鹂鸣翠柳，一行白鹭上青天。窗含西岭千秋雪，门泊东吴万里船""好雨知时节，当春乃发生"，等等。诗人将成都的美、成都的灵动、成都的温暖、成都的寻常景致，一一录入诗中、藏在心里，在他不得不离开成都继续漂泊后，他的草堂及美丽的成都还会一次又一次在梦中出现："万里桥西宅，百花潭北庄。……惜哉形胜地，回首一茫茫！"

有人说成都是一座来了就不想走的城市，无数诗人也像杜甫一样在诗歌里讴歌成都："万里桥边多酒家，游人爱向谁家宿？""濯锦江边两岸花，春风吹浪正淘沙""剑南山水尽清晖，濯锦江边天下稀""二十里中香不断，青羊宫到浣花溪"……

荡漾在清波中的成都人杰地灵。早在公元前141年，文翁就创办了文翁石室，这是全世界最早的学堂之一。大诗人卢照邻在其《文翁讲堂》中写道："锦里淹中馆，岷山稷下亭。……良哉二千石，江汉表遗灵。"源远流长的诗学传统造就了大批文学家和诗人，如司马相如、薛涛、李白、岑参、刘禹锡等。

"锦里名花耳啁啁，花光掩映秋光冷。渔舟一叶荡烟来，划破锦江三尺锦。"

锦城繁花似锦，步步是诗，处处是景，"诗译成都 语话天府"丛书体现的不单单是山水自然、地方风物、茶肆街巷，也展现了最灵动温暖的市井生活，拓展了现代都市的空间诗学与美学价值。成都大学副校长杨玉华教授撰写的《成都最美古诗词一百首：详注精评》出版后好评如潮。本丛书借鉴杨玉华教授的注解，采用中英双语赏析的形式，在挖掘诗意成都的同时，努力用英语讲好中国故事，向世界介绍成都，提升中国读者的国际理解力，提升成都这个大都市的国际形象。

本书的诗歌翻译主译为成都大学外国语学院、海外教育学院特聘研究员，美国新罕布什尔大学孔子学院创始院长王亦歌，参与本书编撰设计的专家和老师还有成都大学海外教育学院兼外国语学院院长杜洁、国际合作与交流处副处长杨茜，以及来自上述两个学院的王利华、林莺、田海稣、熊亭玉、陈欣、周怡乔、杨蓓、牛晓丹、朱玲、郭粒粒、刘颖等诸位老师。本书的英文编辑是美国学者瑚雨然博士。本书的中文赏析由大家共同完成，英文赏析的译者在文中列出。在此基础上，我们为卷二的每首诗歌录制了音频，朗诵者是来自河南沃恩斯文化传播有限公司的臧军湘老师。为方便读者理解，我们精选了五首诗歌制作视频课程，内容由成都大学海外教育学院王舒曼和袁曜两位老师提供。

我国诗歌自古以来就与书法密不可分。本丛书向国外读者介绍成都诗歌的同时，通过突出书画与诗歌相得益彰之美，体现了传统艺术与现代表达形式的融合。成都画院前院长、书法家田旭中，以篆、隶、草、行、楷五种书法风格展示诗歌和作品的部分内容。青年画家田海稣副教授为本书绘制插图，并设计封面。本书独特的艺术风格由上述专家共同打造。

需要说明的是，诗歌之不可译已是老生常谈。马丁·海德格尔（Martin Heidegger，1889—1976）把诗人看成"半人半神"，他认为诗人能通过独特的诗性语词把"道说"转达给世人，而人类也只有通过"倾听"道说才能进入天地人神自由嬉戏的四方域，存在的显现必须在特定境域才能向在场者敞开。若果如海氏所言，那么，想要还原诗人所感受到的那个原始的敞开域里的各种"在场"，并且把这种领会到的道说，也即存在的显现，通过归宿语忠实地传达给读者，就是一个不可能完成的任务。然而，对承载了一个民族的历史文化、审美和情感的重要载体——诗，翻译仍然是必要的，也是我们亟须去做的。对于翻译这门遗憾的艺术再创作来说，我们清醒地认识到译本没有最好，只有更好。本书的翻译只能说是一种新的尝试，在此我们真诚希望有识之士不吝赐教，提出宝贵意见，供再版时修订。

"诗译成都　语话天府"编委会
2022 年 12 月 1 日

From the Editors

The Overseas Education College of Chengdu University, with strong support from university leadership and Center for Language Education and Cooperation of the Ministry of Education of China, assembled a team of experts to produce a collection of poems that best represent Chengdu. Four sizable volumes, containing 100 poems dedicated to Chengdu—in both their original Chinese and in translation—will be published successively.

Chengdu Plain is hailed as the "land of heaven," thanks to a booming agricultural sector and a warm, moist climate. Home to a close-knit multiethnic community, it is of enormous beauty and boasts robust economic health. Famous poet Li Bai effusively extolled these riches in ten poems about the emperor's visit to the city. One of them reads, "Heaven has lavishly endowed Chengdu/with tens of thousands of picturesque residences./Its grass, trees and cloudy mountains vibrant as satin embroidery/surpassing the Qin Plain in all its glory."

Equally inspiring are the many artifacts recently unearthed at the Sanxingdui Ruins, proof that sophisticated techniques of crafting bronze and jade ware were developed in remote antiquity on the Chengdu Plain. A variety of fascinating traditional handicrafts emerged later, which also were written into ancient poems, for example, "Praised for their richness and density/Shu silk hibiscuses are plucked from the crashing waves," and "They open as if carried by the wind/fully unfurling into a crescent moon. /Their jade handles carry age-old tradition/as those of the Han Dynasty court." The handicrafts portrayed in these two excerpts are Shu brocade and fans, respectively.

Chengdu thrived on the nourishment of the

Min River, eventually evolving into the "land of heaven." Its growing prosperity was attributed to Dujiangyan, an irrigation project that was an engineering feat at the time. As poet Li Tiaoyuan's poem attests, "Since the golden dike was built/three prefectures have shared its water… Tens of thousands now harvest bountiful rice/fragrance eternally permeates the plain above." Since its construction two millennia ago, snow water from Min Mountain continues to be harnessed to irrigate crops on the vast Chengdu Plain. The variety of plants grown also encouraged varied handicrafts, for example Xue Tao Paper, a charming type of paper coveted by literati and named after its creator. A poet once wrote, "Xue Tao's poems bloom with spring colors/ten styles of paper in five colors are a marvel." Another example of an artisanal artifact is Shu brocade, described in verses from two poems: "White snow run-off deepens to a dragon green/thousands of brocades are rinsed along River Wen," and "A girl snips a pair of mandarin ducks from brocade./Cast mid-stream, they rival the sunset's glory." Various cultures also emerged on the plain, among them pub culture, depicted in these verses: "The Brocade City is crowded with beautiful women/they sell their rice liquor from behind earthen bars," and "The daughter of Zhuo resides by the Brocade River/her tavern pennant askew on lush new green./People seek her not only for strong liquor/a cup of cold water is just as

intoxicating." The city also was renowned for its local culinary culture: "The freckled Lady Chen has her fame far and wide/as the tofu she cooks is most divine./By the Wanfu Bridge her store curtain flutters/folks stop in to get drunk on spring rice wine." These are among the generous gifts that Chengdu's snow-covered mountains have bestowed on the people around Min River and its countless tributaries, River Jin, River Qingyi, Huanhua Stream, etc. Chengdu's poetry resonates with this rich inheritance.

In these verses—"Towering mansions crowd this city/trees verdant green in winter./Clamoring bustle near and far/with flutes and pipes resounding endlessly"—Du Fu recorded his first impression of Chengdu when he fled here from Tianshui. Riveted by the bustling and lovely city he encountered, the poet decided to settle next to Huanhua Stream ("Flower Rinsing Brook"), initiating what would be the most peaceful and comfortable four years in his life. Du Fu is the reason why Chengdu can proudly claim some of the most-cited Chinese verses: "The twilight illuminates the wet reds/flowers cloaking the Brocade City"; "Fish hurdle in mild drizzle/swallows slant in gentle breezes";"Twin yellow orioles sing among willows green/a trail of white egrets climb to the azure sky./Through the window, the Western Hill's eternal snow peaks/outside the door, the

Eastern Wu's vessels from a myriad *li*"; and "A good rain knows the season/nourishing in spring it descends." His poems provide an account of everything that the poet held dear in Chengdu—its beauty, appeal, affections and everyday affairs. After Du Fu was forced to leave Chengdu, returning to a wandering, unsettled life, the cottage he had lived in and the beautiful city itself kept reappearing in his dreams. "Alas my splendid hometown,/in a vast haze of memory?"

Some say that once arrived Chengdu, you will never want to leave. This is certainly true for numerous poets, who, like Du Fu, celebrated Chengdu's well-known locations in poems:"Taverns circle Wanli Bridge/ Where to lodge? Wonder the travelers"; "Along the Brocade Rinsing River/flowers bloom, the spring breeze carries waves over the sand" ; "The landscape of Jiannan is exquisite/surpassed in grandeur only along the Zhuojin River"; and "For twenty *li* the fragrance lingered/from the Qingyang Temple to the Huanhua Stream."

A great city fosters great minds. As early as 141 BC, Wen Weng started one of the world's earliest schools in Chengdu, "Wen Weng Shi Shi"(or "Wen Weng Stone Academy"). Lu Zhaolin, another accomplished poet, wrote about it in his work: "Here was once the Center of Confucianism in Jinli/and a draw for scholars to the Min Mountains... I pay homage to the former governor-scholar/ whose legacy persists in the Han and Yangzi regions." Chengdu's long-standing poetic tradition has nurtured an abundance of literati and poets, such as Sima Xiangru, Xue Tao, Li Bai, Cen Shen, and Liu Yuxi.

"The Brocade City's blooms are luminous and bright/they shine through the chilly autumn light./A lone fishing junk floats from the mist/piercing the sinuous brocade silk of River Jin."

In the Brocade City, poets need only look around for inspiration: natural scenery, folktales, tea houses and street scenes. All of these elements appear in this series *One Hundred of the Most Beautiful Poems of Chengdu: Land of Poetry and Abundance.* More importantly, this set captures local folk culture, which represents the most significant source of appeal and interest, expanding the poetic importance and aesthetic value of modern cities. The poems and their commentary by colleagues, the latter based on annotations provided by Yang Yuhua, Vice President of Chengdu University, author of a highly rated and best-selling collection of what are considered the one hundred most beautiful verses about Chengdu, are printed in both Chinese and English for several reasons: to generate interest in poems about Chengdu; to tell Chinese stories well in English; to introduce Chengdu to the world; to raise the international understanding of Chinese readers; and to rebrand Chengdu as a culturally progressive cosmopolitan.

Wang Yige, founding director of the Confucius Institute at the University of New Hampshire and research fellow from Chengdu University's College of Foreign Languages and Cultures and College of Overseas Education, is the lead translator of the poems. Also involved in their compilation are colleagues from the College of Overseas Education and College of Foreign Languages and Cultures, including Professor and Dean Du Jie, Deputy Director Yang Xi of Office of International Cooperation and Exchange, Wang Lihua, Lin Ying, Tian Haisu, Xiong Tingyu, Chen Xin, Zhou Yiqiao, Yang Bei, Niu Xiaodan, Zhu Ling, Guo Lili, and Liu Ying. The English editor is Dr. Lorraine Hu of U.S. All teachers helped contribute to the Chinese digests. The translators are listed individually in the book. Based on this, we recorded audio for each poem in volume 2, and the reciter is Teacher Zang Junxiang from Henan Wones Culture Communication Co., Ltd. For the convenience of reader's understanding, we selected five poems to produce video courses, which were provided by two teachers, Wang Shuman and Yuan Yao, from College of Overseas Education of Chengdu University.

Poetry is traditionally associated with calligraphy. This new series of four books which introduces foreign readers to Chengdu's poetry reflects the fusion of traditional arts and modern forms of expression by highlighting the beauty of pairing calligraphy and painting in support to poetry. Tian Xuzhong, a calligrapher and former director of the Chengdu Art Academy, presents some poems and excerpts of others using five styles of calligraphy: seal, clerical, cursive, semi-cursive and standard. Each book has illustrations by the well-known young artist and Fine Arts associate professor Tian Haisu, who also designed the covers. The contributions from all the experts above give the book a unique artistic style.

It should be noted that it is already a cliché that poetry is untranslatable from one language to another. Heidegger sees poets as demigods. He believes that poets can relay "what they have heard" to the public through the unique language of poetry, and only by "listening" can humans be part of the "Gathering of the Fourfold," where sky and earth, divinities and mortals dwell together all at once in Spiel-Raum (free-space). The manifestation of (divine, spiritual) Being discloses itself to those present beings only under a given horizon. If Heidegger is right, it would be impossible to restore the "presence (presencing)" felt/ experienced by the poet in the original disclosure field (horizon), and faithfully convey the manifestation of Being, through the target language (or language into which poems are translated), to foreign readers. That being said, translating poetry for "the other side" remains an indispensable undertaking. After all, poetry does speak for the history, culture, aesthetics and emotions of a nation. All of us included in bringing this series to life are mindful of a regrettable truth: translation, essentially an art of recreation, is by nature imperfect. Translators therefore must always strive to do better. This series is another such attempt. We value all constructive feedback as we look to future reprints.

The editorial committee of *One Hundred of the Most Beautiful Poems of Chengdu: Land of Poetry and Abundance*
December 1, 2022

目录
CONTENTS

002　荆门浮舟望蜀江　　　　　　　　　　　　　　　李白
　　　Afloat near Jingmen admiring River Shu　　　　Li Bai

006　成都府　　　　　　　　　　　　　　　　　　　杜甫
　　　Chengdu Prefect　　　　　　　　　　　　　　Du Fu

010　登楼　　　　　　　　　　　　　　　　　　　　杜甫
　　　Tower ascending　　　　　　　　　　　　　　Du Fu

015　万里桥　　　　　　　　　　　　　　　　　　　岑参
　　　Wanli Bridge　　　　　　　　　　　　　　　Cen Shen

019　玩半开花赠皇甫郎中（节选）　　　　　　　　　　白居易
　　　To Huangpu the Court Official about flowers in partial bloom　　Bai Juyi

023　锦城写望　　　　　　　　　　　　　　　　　　高骈
　　　Viewing the Brocade City from a tower　　　　Gao Pian

028　十二月十一日视筑堤　　　　　　　　　　　　　陆游
　　　On a dike construction site on the eleventh of the lunar twelfth month　　Lu You

032　归蜀　　　　　　　　　　　　　　　　　　　　虞集
　　　A trip back to Shu　　　　　　　　　　　　　Yu Ji

036　客至　　　　　　　　　　　　　　　　　　　　杜甫
　　　Delighted at an unexpected visit by the county magistrate Cui (Guest arrives)　　Du Fu

041　竹枝词九首 · 其四　　　　　　　　　　　　　刘禹锡
　　　Nine Bamboo Songs-No.4　　　　　　　　　　Liu Yuxi

045　　乞彩笺歌　　　　　　　　　　　　　　　　　韦庄
　　　Song of begging for handcrafted colored note-papers　　Wei Zhuang

049　　浣花泛舟和韵　　　　　　　　　　　　　　　吕陶
　　　Responding to someone's poem from a boat on Huanhua Stream　　Lü Tao

054　　和子由《蚕市》　　　　　　　　　　　　　苏轼
　　　In response to Ziyou's poem about "Silk Festival"　　Su Shi

058　　夜闻浣花江声甚壮　　　　　　　　　　　　陆游
　　　On hearing the mighty Huanhua Stream torrent at night　　Lu You

062　　青羊宫小饮赠道士　　　　　　　　　　　　陆游
　　　To the Daoist priest of the Qingyang Temple after tea　　Lu You

067　　锦城竹枝词　　　　　　　　　　　　　　　杨燮
　　　Bamboo songs of the Brocade City　　Yang Xie

071　　花会场竹枝词　　　　　　　　　　　　　　谢家驹
　　　A bamboo song from the Flower Festival　　Xie Jiaju

075　　丈人山　　　　　　　　　　　　　　　　　杜甫
　　　Mount Elder (Mount Qingcheng)　　Du Fu

080　　到蜀后记途中经历　　　　　　　　　　　　雍陶
　　　Recalling the journey along the way after arriving in Shu　　Yong Tao

084　　鹊桥仙·乘槎归去　　　　　　　　　　　　苏轼
　　　To the tune of Reunion on the Magpie Bridge-Boarding a bamboo raft　　Su Shi
　　　on return (Responding to Su Jian's poem on Chinese Valentine's Day)

088　　题黄筌芙蓉图　　　　　　　　　　　　　　赵构
　　　Responding to Huang Quan's beautiful painting of hibiscus　　Zhao Gou

093　　蔬食戏书　　　　　　　　　　　　　　　　陆游
　　　Ribbing at my vegetarian diet　　Lu You

097　　怀锦水居止·其二　　　　　　　　　　　　杜甫
　　　Recollecting my cottage by the Brocade Water No.2　　Du Fu

101　　杜鹃城　　　　　　　　　　　　　　　　　卫道凝
　　　The Cuckoo City　　Wei Daoning

105　　和青城题壁诗　　　　　　　　　　　　　　骆成骧
　　　Responding to the poem inscribed on the wall of Qingcheng Temple　　Luo Chengxiang

荆门浮舟望蜀江

〔唐〕李白

春水月峡来，浮舟望安极。

正是桃花流，依然锦江色。

江色绿且明，茫茫与天平。

逶迤巴山尽，摇曳楚云行。

雪照聚沙雁，花飞出谷莺。

芳洲却已转，碧树森森迎。

流目浦烟夕，扬帆海月生。

江陵识遥火，应到渚宫城。

Afloat near Jingmen admiring River Shu

Li Bai
Tang Dynasty

Vernal water runs from the Moon Gorge

here afloat, where is the river's end?

Peach blossoms drift by

the Brocade River must also be aglow.

The river water crystal and green

as it merges into the distant sky.

Mount Ba winds, coming to an end

Chu clouds billow upwards.

Wild geese flock under snowy reflections

from a ravine, orioles frolic among blooms.

Along the lush sandbars my boat turns

flourishing trees line to greet me.

Sunset's glory fills the endless sky

the Moon rises with my hoisting sail.

Lights gleam from distant Jiangling

the town of Zhugong must be ahead.

"酒入豪肠，七分酿成了月光，余下的三分啸成剑气，绣口一吐就半个盛唐。"（余光中《寻李白》）遥望我国浩瀚璀璨的诗歌星空，李白无疑是最夺目的那颗星，所谓"笔落惊风雨，诗成泣鬼神"。诗人一生佳作迭出，许多诗作兴到神会，信笔而成。自20多岁仗剑去国，辞亲远游，李白再未回到故乡。然而故土之情却终生萦绕，随年岁渐长而乡关情深。当他见千里江陵，闻两岸猿声，思乡之情不禁油然而生。春水桃花，楚云巴山，蜀江锦水，芳州碧树，一一涌上心头，加之遇赦后心情轻松愉悦，故触景生情成此名篇，令后人吟咏千年。

"Mix wine with gallantry, seven parts brew moonlight, the rest three gleam sword shimmer. Half a prosperous Tang Dynasty unfurls whenever he chants his elegant poetry." ("Quest for Li Bai, " Yu Guangzhong). In the vast starry sky of Chinese poetry, Li Bai is undoubtedly the most dazzling. "His poetry brush unleashes wind and rain, and poems move gods in heaven." Li Bai penned numerous masterpieces throughout his life, and many were drafted in one go, fueled by inspiration and zest. At his twenties, Li Bai bid farewell to his loved ones and set off from his hometown, accompanied only by his sword. Although he never returned, his nostalgia lingered and stayed with him throughout his life. As his homesickness aged with him, he couldn't help but recall his hometown when he gazed at the distant Jiangling far down the river, with monkeys howling along the riverbanks. Peach blossom petals floating on vernal currents, the clouds of Chu and the mountains of Ba, the beautiful rivers of Shu, the lush trees on verdant embankments, all flashed by and came into his mind. Coupled with elation after his amnesty, he wrote this masterpiece in a fusion of emotions with natural surroundings evoked by his memories of the past. This piece has become a cherished one, chanted through generations. (By Wang Lihua)

春水月峽來　浮舟望安極
正是桃花流　依然錦江色
江色綠且明　茫茫與天平
逶迤巴山盡　搖曳雲間行
雪照聚沙鷗　花飛出谷鶯
芳洲卻已轉　碧樹森森迎
流目浦煙夕　揚帆海月生
江陵識遙火　應到渚宮城

李白荆門浮舟望蜀江

歲次壬寅夏满昆平書於成都

成都府 chéng dū fǔ

〔唐〕杜甫 táng dù fǔ

翳翳桑榆日，照我征衣裳。
yì yì sāng yú rì　zhào wǒ zhēng yī shang

我行山川异，忽在天一方。
wǒ xíng shān chuān yì　hū zài tiān yì fāng

但逢新人民，未卜见故乡。
dàn féng xīn rén mín　wèi bǔ jiàn gù xiāng

大江东流去，游子去日长。
dà jiāng dōng liú qù　yóu zǐ qù rì cháng

曾城填华屋，季冬树木苍。
zēng chéng tián huá wū　jì dōng shù mù cāng

喧然名都会，吹箫间笙簧。
xuān rán míng dū huì　chuī xiāo jiàn shēng huáng

信美无与适，侧身望川梁。
xìn měi wú yǔ shì　cè shēn wàng chuān liáng

鸟雀夜各归，中原杳茫茫。
niǎo què yè gè guī　zhōng yuán yǎo máng máng

初月出不高，众星尚争光。
chū yuè chū bù gāo　zhòng xīng shàng zhēng guāng

自古有羁旅，我何苦哀伤！
zì gǔ yǒu jī lǚ　wǒ hé kǔ āi shāng

Chengdu Prefect

Du Fu
Tang Dynasty

The setting sun fades over mulberry and elm trees, its afterglow shrouding my
traveler's clothes.

Through different mountains and rivers, I am suddenly under an unfamiliar sky.

Not a single acquaintance have I met, nor do I know when I'm homeward bound.

The mighty river southerly flows, so are my wandering days endless.

Towering mansions crowd the city, trees a lush green even in winter.

Clamor and bustle throughout the metropolis, with flutes following pipes irregularly.

Bucolic is this, in the flourishing city, I gaze aside at the mountains afar.

Homing birds dash by at evenfall, the war at the heartland rages on.

The crescent moon hangs low in the sky, with twinkling stars vying for brilliance

Many have drifted before, why let despondence take over me!

755 年，安史之乱爆发，大唐王朝由盛而衰。三年之后，杜甫为躲避战乱，应好友严武的邀请，历尽艰难险阻，拖家带口来到成都。

《成都府》为诗人初到成都时所作。满目疮痍、烽火连天的长安与安闲平静、富庶繁华的成都形成巨大反差，令诗人震惊，甚至有些手足无措。归巢的夜鸟引发诗人有家难回的痛苦，而暗淡的新月与众星争光的夜空更让诗人联想到朝廷沦陷后群雄并起、中原板荡的国家命运，一腔家国情怀悲愤难抑，今昔对比之中无语凝噎。诗作借物抒怀，充分表达了诗人仁民爱物的伟大人文主义情怀。

After the An-Shi Rebellion broke out in 755, the Tang Dynasty went from prosperity into decline. Three years later, at the invitation of his good friend Yan Wu, Du Fu brought his family to Chengdu after considerable hardships on the way.

Du Fu wrote the piece "Chengdu Prefect" after their arrival in Chengdu. The stark contrast between the total devastation and raging flames of war in Chang'an, and a leisurely peaceful and prosperous Chengdu shocked the poet. The birds at dusk, returning to their roosts, reminded the poet about his own displacement far from home. The dim crescent moon and stars vying for brilliance in the night sky reminded the poet of the fate of the country and of how all warlords fought for dominance in the power vacuum following the decline of the court. From his love for his country to the grief and indignation brought on by conflict, the shocking contrast between the present and the past made him speechless. Thus, in expressing his feelings through other means such as poetry, the poem reveals the poet's universal love through his great humanistic feelings for all. (By Wang Lihua)

籍：桑榆日照我征衣裳我

行山川异态鱼在天一方但鱼新

人民束卜兄故乡　大江东流

去游子青春曹城填华屋

季冬树木苍喧然名都会吹

簫间笙簧信美无与适侧

身望川谏鸟雀夜呑归

中原書疏：初月出不高眠

星尚争光自古宿旅我

何苦哀伤

壬寅成都居

雷思齐书

登楼 (dēng lóu)

〔唐〕杜甫 (táng dù fǔ)

花近高楼伤客心，

万方多难此登临。

锦江春色来天地，

玉垒浮云变古今。

北极朝廷终不改，

西山寇盗莫相侵。

可怜后主还祠庙，

日暮聊为梁甫吟。

Tower ascending

Du Fu
Tang Dynasty

Flowers from the tower arouse my sorrow

as I come to ascend in time's great turmoil.

Spring along River Jin comes on its own

the clouds above Mount Yulei ever change with time.

The royal court is inviolable as the North Star

raiders beyond western mountains dare not invade.

A sigh to the last emperor's shrine

I cannot help but chant *Liangfu* at dusk.

此诗写于诗人客居成都的第五个年头，即 764 年。锦城春晓，风暖蓉城，莺声燕语。诗人登上高楼，眼前的无边春色并未使诗人有些许快乐，反而引发诗人对故土的伤心感喟。春色依旧而人间物是人非，山河虽在而江山残破不堪，诗人睹物伤感，思绪联翩，黍离之悲迭次循环，朝代兴衰变化无常。虽唐王朝政权还算稳固，吐蕃的入侵也未能使之动摇；虽自己客居他乡，但仍情系家国，愿效法诸葛亮，辅佐朝廷，致君尧舜，再淳风俗。无边春色与满怀悲伤相对照，反向映衬中令人似乎看到一位沧桑老人举目远眺、驻足沉思、壮志未酬的身影。诗之感人至此，益信"诗圣"之誉不妄。

This poem was written in 764, the fifth year after Du Fu arrived in Chengdu. Spring had arrived in the Brocade City with warm breezes sweeping over the city full of hibiscus, as orioles and swallows sang. The poet came to ascend a high tower, yet, instead of being cheered up by the glorious scene of spring in front his eyes, the poet couldn't help but lament for his homeland. All the hues of spring were still the same but other things had permanently changed– a broken country with only its mountains and rivers unchanged. The poet, sentimental at the scene, became lost in his thoughts; the prosperity and decline of a dynasty or kingdom, he mused, were ever-cyclical. The Tang Dynasty then was still somewhat stable, and even the invasion from the west had failed to substantially affect the court. Although now a wanderer far away from the heartland, the poet still felt for his homeland with the wish to follow Zhuge Liang's footsteps to serve the court, and to make His Majesty a sage king for a renewed, civilized society. The spring scene in the poem, juxtaposed with his grief, depicts a weathered senior gazing afar while lost in his thoughts, and reveals all the detestations, and unfulfilled dreams through the view of his past. The complexity of emotions touched upon by this poem underscores Du Fu's reputation as "the sage poet." (By Wang Lihua)

独上高楼临远
山万叠方为难题
烟雨暗江山黛色
林下地无尘浮
空堂寂寂山静
玉峰云破西山露
濛濛林梢可情
石立画初寒日
苍茫 为梁
而吟

拟甫蒼我
乙未山满溪三〇
思亮中秋书于半舟

万里桥

〔唐〕岑参

成都与维扬，

相去万里地。

沧江东流疾，

帆去如鸟翅。

楚客过此桥，

东看尽垂泪。

Wanli Bridge

Cen Shen
Tang Dynasty

Chengdu and Weiyang sit apart

at different ends of a rainbow.

The mighty river rushes south

distant sails glide like birds' wings.

Any dweller from Chu crossing this bridge

has tears streaming down, as they gaze eastward.

赏析

成都平原自古就有"天府"之称，赖于山水便利，物产富饶。而扬州（维扬）亦有"淮左名都"之谓。两地均有地便形胜之利。尤其唐朝时期，各领两域繁荣昌盛之首，又有水路交通之便，故有"扬一益二"的说法。

岑参，湖北荆州人，唐边塞诗领军人物，善于描绘塞上风光和战争景象。此诗为诗人送别友人回维扬之作，朋友归家团圆，自己仍客居外地，由人到己，难免黯然神伤。送别之际，江水滔滔，东流无语，"楚客"伤神。"无情未必真豪杰，只是未到伤心处"，故乡之思，永远是中国人内心最软弱的一角。

Appreciation

Chengdu Plain has been known as "the land of abundance" since ancient times, thanks to its rich resources and products, while Yangzhou (Weiyang) is known as "the festive city left of Huai River." Both cities have advantages due to their convenient and preferable geographic locations. During the Tang Dynasty, both cities were the most prosperous in their regions, and coupled with the convenience of the canal age traffic, were referenced in the saying, "Yangzhou the top city and Yizhou the second."

Cen Shen, a native of Jingzhou city in Hubei Province, was a leading author of frontier poetry in the Tang Dynasty and known for his depictions of frontier scenery and war scenes. This poem is about seeing off a friend back to Weiyang. With his friends returning home for family reunions, he was left far away from home and inevitably felt gloomy. At the time of farewell, as the surging river flows east, the "dweller from Chu" is depicted in silent grief. "A true hero may seem without affection, as he is yet to display grief." Nostalgia will forever be the softest spot in the hearts of every Chinese. (By Zhu Ling)

成都与维扬
相去万里地
沧江东流疾
帆去如飞鸟

楚客留此
篙师指东看
无源

岁在辛亥暮春之初
己丑年书

玩半开花赠皇甫郎中（节选）

〔唐〕白居易

勿讶春来晚，无嫌花发迟。

人怜全盛日，我爱半开时。

紫蜡黏为蒂，红苏点作蕤。

成都新夹缬[1]，梁汉碎胭脂。

---

1 始于秦汉、盛行于唐宋的一种古老的印染技术。

To Huangpu the Court Official about flowers in partial bloom

Bai Juyi[1]
Tang Dynasty

Worry not about the belated arrival of spring

nor be disappointed at spring's late blooming.

People cherish full blossoming

I prefer them in partial bloom.

Their calyxes as purple wax

pistils and stamens are red perilla.

As if Chengdu is adorned with trendiest brocade (Jiaxie)[2]

topped with Lianghan's best blush.

1　Bai Juyi (772−846), courtesy name Letian, also known as "a lay Buddhist on Mount Xiang," is one of the greatest realistic poets in the Tang Dynasty. Bai Juyi's poems cover a wide range of themes using various styles and plain language. He is known as the "Magician of Poetry" and "Master of Poetry." His poems reflected the social life of the mid-Tang Dynasty. Through his literature, he advocated that articles should be written for the time, and songs and poems should be composed based on facts.

2　Jiaxie was an ancient printing and dyeing technology developed in the Qin and Han dynasties and popularized in the Tang and Song dynasties.

常人爱花，多喜全盛之姿，但姹紫嫣红固然风华绝代，却也是盛极而衰的开始。经历了人生跌宕起伏的白居易，似乎更能体会含苞半露的意味。或许是它似开未开的蕴藉风姿？或许是充满希望与未来的期待？或许是半全之盛、物极必反的中国古老哲理？总之，一首小诗，由花而人，却有深厚意味，常言"月满则亏，水满则溢"，或许半开、不满才是最美的风景。

成都丝织业发达，蜀锦蜀绣闻名于世，夹缬技术及图案形式也独步全国。在诗句中，诗人用成都的夹缬来比喻美丽的鲜花。

Most people love flowers when they are in full bloom. Though colorful and luxuriant with peerless elegance, they mark the beginning of boom and bust. With too many ups and downs in life, Bai Juyi seemed to better understand flowers in partial bloom. Was it for the contained grace to be displayed? Or the hope and expectations for the future imbedded within? Or was it the ancient Chinese philosophy behind partial blooms that all things turn to their opposites when reaching extremes, and that things eventually go from zenith to wane? To sum up, from flowers to people, this short poem has a profound meaning. As the saying goes, "the moon waxes only to wane, water brims only to overflow." Perhaps to be in partial bloom is the best scene.

Chengdu is famous for its Shu brocade and embroidery due to its developed silk industry. Its Jiaxie technology as well as the patterned designs are also renowned in China. In the poem, the poet used "Jiaxie" to refer to beautiful flowers. (By Zhu Ling)

忽访春日来晚
气娇花尝辽远
人惭金盛日我
爱半闻时紫
蜿黏为蒂红
苏黑作蕤成
却新夹缬梁
汉碎胭脂
白屏易玩半闻花
赠皇冒郎中
壬寅初夏思华书

锦城写望

〔唐〕高骈

蜀江波影碧悠悠，

四望烟花匝郡楼。

不会人家多少锦，

春来尽挂树梢头。

Viewing the Brocade City from a tower

Gao Pian[1]
Tang Dynasty

The green Shu River ripples on and on

looking around, misty blooms circle the tower below.

A myriad of brocade pieces

drape branches in the glory of spring.

---

1   Gao Pian (821−887), was a famous general and poet in late Tang Dynasty. In his youth, he studied and researched books of military arts, in addition to his love for literature. In the year of 875, he was appointed the prefect of Chengdu, as well as the military commander of Jiannan Xichuan.

赏析

公务之暇，高骈登高远眺，但见锦江碧波荡漾，两岸繁花弥漫。锦江作为成都的母亲河，滋润了成都的山水，成就了悠久发达的织锦业。西南富庶唯"天府"，山川秀美看锦城。作为成都最高的军事行政长官，高骈为成都的风物人情锦绣江山而陶醉，为能镇守西南名城而自豪。其文才武略，"乘醉听箫鼓，吟赏烟霞"的雅趣之中，坐拥十万精兵，舍我其谁的豪迈之情则非寻常诗人所能体会。

Appreciation

Off duty during his tenure in Sichuan, the poet climbed a mountain for a sight of the undulating green ripples of Jinjiang River (Shu River) and profuse blossoms along the embankments. As the mother river of Chengdu, Jinjiang River helps Chengdu shine with its natural beauty as well as its lasting and booming brocade industry. Chengdu overlooks the southwest in prosperity with its natural beauty unrivaled. Gao Pian, as the highest military and administrative officer of Chengdu, was charmed by its customs and natural beauty and was also proud to be in charge of this festival city of the southwest. Well-versed in literary and military arts, Gao Pian had refined tastes and would "tipsily tap along to flutes and drums while exalting the glory of misty sunbeams." As a general in command of a hundred thousand well-trained soldiers, his dashing valiancy and a sense of leadership was rarely found in other poets. (By Xiong Tingyu)

蜀江波影碧悠悠四望煙花匝郡樓不會人家多少錦春來畫橋楨頭

高騈錦城寫望
壬辰初夏翠華書

十二月十一日视筑堤

〔宋〕陆游

江水来自蛮夷中，五月六月声摩空。

巨鱼穹龟牙须雄，欲取阛市为龙宫。

横堤百丈卧霁虹，始谁筑此东平公。

今年乐哉适岁丰，吏不相倚勇赴功。

西山大竹织万笼，船舸载石来亡穷。

横陈屹立相叠重，置力尤在水庙东。

我登高原相其冲，一盾可受百箭攻。

蜿蜿其长高隆隆，截如长城限羌戎。

安得椽笔记始终，插江石崖坚可砻。

On a dike construction site
on the eleventh of the lunar twelfth month

Lu You
Song Dynasty

Torrents rush from nomadic lands, in May and June they rumble by.

As if giant fish and tortoises race along, to make the city center a dragon's palace.

A colossal dike stretches like a rainbow, the one started this mighty project is a true hero.

This year's harvest brings peace and joy, as all volunteer for dike fortification.

Thousands of western mountain bamboo cages are filled with boulders, carried by boats nonstop.

Criss-crossed, they stack up high east of the water dragon temple, secured with double piles.

I ascend a hill to judge its strength, is it surely will withstand any assault.

The dike stretches and rises high, like the Great Wall holding back the nomads.

How I wish to record this great deed, to show that when united, even nature yields.

陆游生于北宋灭亡之际，少年时即深受家庭爱国思想的熏陶。因坚持抗金，屡遭主和派排斥。1171 年，陆游应四川宣抚使王炎之邀，投身军旅，任职于南郑幕府。次年，幕府解散，陆游奉诏入蜀。这首诗写于 1173 年，诗人亲自参与了这次筑堤防洪活动。

诗歌首先以夸张手法写洪水来势汹汹，波涛滚滚，众水横流，巨浪滔天。再写勤劳勇敢的川民不畏艰险，抗争自然的力量与勇气。最后诗人登高而望，堤坝蜿蜒高耸，巍然矗立，宛如长城一般，抵挡了滔滔洪水的侵犯，护卫了两岸百姓的安宁。这是人类与大自然的搏斗，是巴蜀人民无畏精神的华章。

Lu You was born into a very patriotic family at the end of the northern Song Dynasty. The idea of serving his motherland was deeply rooted in his heart. Due to his patriotic irredentist stance against the invading Jurchens, he was often dismissed by those who hoped to make peace through negotiation and concession. In the year of 1171, he was offered a post in the Nanzheng Headquarters by Wangyan, who was in charge of Sichuan Province. In the next year, when the headquarters was dissolved, Lu You received a court decree to serve in Sichuan. This poem was written in 1173 when Lu You participated in the fortification of a dike built to tame flooding.

Through dramatization the poem begins with the peril of a violent flood with rolling surges and raging colossal waves. Then the poem shifts to the strength and courage of the valiant people of Sichuan in braving hardships and facing the power of nature. Finally, Lu You climbed high and looked afar: the dam meanders and rises in splendor, like a towering Great Wall holding firmly against the invasion of floods, protecting the peace and safety of people along the river banks. The poem depicts a battle between humans and nature, a glorious record of the people of Sichuan's dauntless spirit. (By Xiong Tingyu)

江水來自蠻
東中五月六月
聲摩空巨魚
寧驅牙須鬣
漁取閣市多龍
宫横堤百丈臥
霜虹姑姑築此
東平公今年樂
裁通歲晏宝变
不相倚勇赴功
西山大竹織萬籠
船航載石來已
窜撐陳屹立相
疊重置力尤在
水廟東我登高
原相甚冲一百
可受百箭攻蜿
蜿其長高隆成
如長城限羌戎
安游榜筆記
此樑挿江石崖
堅可磨
陸游十二月十二視
筆硯
王寶聖文田華書

归蜀

〔元〕虞集

我 到 成 都 住 五 日 ， 驷 马 桥 下 春 水 生 。

过 江 相 送 荷 主 意 ， 还 乡 不 留 非 我 情 。

鸬 鹚 轻 筏 下 溪 足 ， 鹦 鹉 小 窗 呼 客 名 。

赖 得 郫 筒 酒 易 醉 ， 夜 深 冲 雨 汉 州 城 。

A trip back to Shu

Yu Ji[1]
Yuan Dynasty

I have but five days in Chengdu

as the spring current rises under the Bridge of Four Horses.

A friend came across the river to greet me

But with official duties I must depart.

Cormorants dive from a bamboo raft on a stream

a parakeet chants a guest's name by a window.

It is a blessing to get tipsy with Pitong rice wine

as a downpour carries my boat to Hanzhou late at night.

---

1   Yu Ji (1272−1348) was a famous scholar of the Yuan Dynasty. Coming from a well−known family of literature tradition, Yu Ji himself was also learned and talented with equal fame in prose and poetry, and ranked among the top four poets of the Yuan Dynasty.

"蜀人偏爱蜀江山"，虞集祖籍为成都仁寿（今眉山市仁寿县），他虽非生于成都，但对锦绣故园却一直魂牵梦绕，朝夕难忘。某年，终于得到"代祀西岳"差事，夙愿得偿，何其快哉。于是他迂道还乡，遂平生之愿。驷马桥下春水涟漪，游子归家草木深情，见鸬鹚渔舟何等亲切，听鹦鹉鸣叫也似挽留……但人在宦途，身不由己，短短几天，倏忽而过，转眼又要离开。与亲友洒泪而别，他感谢友人渡江相送的盛情，感喟自己过家不留的无奈。

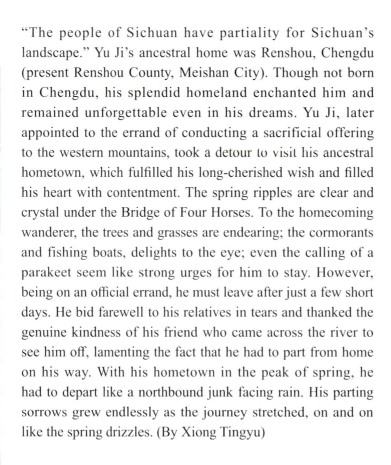

"The people of Sichuan have partiality for Sichuan's landscape." Yu Ji's ancestral home was Renshou, Chengdu (present Renshou County, Meishan City). Though not born in Chengdu, his splendid homeland enchanted him and remained unforgettable even in his dreams. Yu Ji, later appointed to the errand of conducting a sacrificial offering to the western mountains, took a detour to visit his ancestral hometown, which fulfilled his long-cherished wish and filled his heart with contentment. The spring ripples are clear and crystal under the Bridge of Four Horses. To the homecoming wanderer, the trees and grasses are endearing; the cormorants and fishing boats, delights to the eye; even the calling of a parakeet seem like strong urges for him to stay. However, being on an official errand, he must leave after just a few short days. He bid farewell to his relatives in tears and thanked the genuine kindness of his friend who came across the river to see him off, lamenting the fact that he had to part from home on his way. With his hometown in the peak of spring, he had to depart like a northbound junk facing rain. His parting sorrows grew endlessly as the journey stretched, on and on like the spring drizzles. (By Xiong Tingyu)

我到成都信五日

驰马桥下春水生

过江相送荷主意

还乡不减非我情

鸬鹚孤筏下溪口

鹦鹉小槎呼客名

赖游郫筒酒易

醉卧深冲西汉州

城

崖集归蜀

壬寅冬月

田耀中 画于成都

客至

〔唐〕杜甫

舍南舍北皆春水，但见群鸥日日来。

花径不曾缘客扫，蓬门今始为君开。

盘飧市远无兼味，樽酒家贫只旧醅。

肯与邻翁相对饮，隔篱呼取尽余杯。

Delighted at an unexpected visit
by the county magistrate Cui (Guest arrives)

Du Fu
Tang Dynasty

Vernal currents flow by my cottage to the north and south

flocks of seagulls hover around each day.

The floral path is yet to be swept for guests

my shabby gate wide-flung for you today.

Far from any market, my food is plain

and rice wine muddy with my meager living.

If you do not mind sharing with a neighboring senior,

let us call him over the fence to drink this wine.

唐代诗人多与成都结缘，杜甫与成都缘分最深。这首诗是杜甫所作的一首广为传颂的写成都的诗。安史之乱后，杜甫历经颠沛流离来到成都，在友人资助下，于西郊的浣花溪畔修建了一座草堂并在此定居，由此开始了一段相对安定的生活。诗人淳厚重友，其间时有朋友来往，于是写了不少朋友交往的诗。此诗是杜甫在草堂建成不久后有客来访时所作。南北春水、日日群鸥装点了简陋的草堂，安定的生活给了诗人短暂的悠闲时光，老友新朋的到来自然使杜甫格外喜悦，虽全诗仅仅八句，但盼客、迎客、待客、陪客却写得生动自然。蓬门简陋，旧醅清淡，却抵不住离乱之中友人相聚的真情厚意。草堂，因诗人而生辉；成都，因诗人而增色。

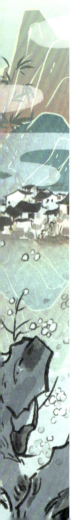

Many poets in the Tang Dynasty had ties with Chengdu, and Du Fu had the deepest attachments. This is one of his most well-known Chengdu poems. Displaced after the An-Shi Rebellion in the Tang Dynasty, Du Fu struggled with destitution and hardships to reach Chengdu. With the help of his friends, he built a thatched cottage and settled down near Huanhua Stream in the western suburbs and started a relatively stable life. Du Fu was faithful and honest to his friends, who frequently visited him; many of his poems are about the visits. Du Fu penned this poem about welcoming a guest shortly after the completion of his cottage. Vernal flows to the north and south and the flocks of seagulls that he witnessed each day added to the charm of his humble cottage. The peaceful and stable life provided a short respite for the poet, and the visits of friends old and new brought him much joy. Although the poem has just eight lines, the descriptions about expecting, welcoming, entertaining, and accompanying guests are vivid and natural. Even though the garden gate was shabby, his rice wine muddy and food plain, they did not detract from the heartfelt sincerity he felt when friends gathered during times of chaos. The thatched cottage is made ever lustrous and Chengdu shines because of Du Fu's poetry. (By Chen Xin)

舍南舍北皆春水
但见群鸥日日来
花径不曾缘客扫
蓬门今始为君开
盘飧市远无兼味
樽酒家贫只旧醅
肯与邻翁相对饮
隔篱呼取尽余杯

杜甫客至
田英章书

竹枝词九首·其四

〔唐〕刘禹锡

日出三竿春雾消，

江头蜀客驻兰桡。

凭寄狂夫书一纸，

家住成都万里桥。

Nine Bamboo Songs– No.4

Liu Yuxi
Tang Dynasty

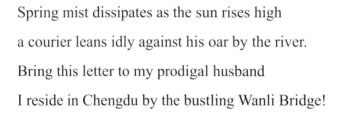

Spring mist dissipates as the sun rises high

a courier leans idly against his oar by the river.

Bring this letter to my prodigal husband

I reside in Chengdu by the bustling Wanli Bridge!

赏析

　　《竹枝词九首》写于822年，是刘禹锡在夔州（今重庆市奉节县）任官时所作。"竹枝词"本是古代四川东部人民口头传唱的一种民歌，人们用鼓和短笛伴奏，边舞边唱。刘禹锡非常喜欢这种民歌，所以采当地民歌曲谱，制成《竹枝词九首》，描写当地的山水风俗或男女爱情。因借用民歌体，所以出语自然，清新活泼，生动流畅，活色生香，充满浓郁的生活气息和鲜明的地方特色。一首小诗，活化出主人公对丈夫的思念和嗔怒交织的情感，泼辣生动，颇有川蜀风格。该诗于唐诗典雅之中另辟蹊径，标志着以朴实语言表达写意中国文化的开始。

Appreciation

"Nine Bamboo Songs" were written by Liu Yuxi in 822 when he was an official in Kuizhou (now Fengjie County, Chongqing City). "Zhuzhi Ci" was originally a form of folk song popular in eastern Sichuan in ancient times. People would dance and sing to the drums and piccolos. Liu Yuxi fell in love with these kinds of folk songs. Adapting the local folk song scores, he wrote nine poems describing the local landscape, customs, and the love between men and women. In folk song style, the verses are natural, unique and lively, vivid and fluent, and full of the rich flavor of life and distinctive local characteristics. The short poem vividly portrays a woman's feelings of love mixed with discontent for her husband as bold and adamant, straightforward and frank in typical Sichuan style. This style, different from the elegant Tang poetry, marks the beginning of expressing poetic Chinese culture in more casual prose. (By Chen Xin)

日出三竿春

霧消江頭蜀

客駐蘭橈恨

寄得夫書一紙

家住成都萬

里橋

劉禹錫竹枝詞

九首其四

壬辰小滿日

思旭中書於成都

乞彩笺歌

〔唐〕韦庄

浣花溪上如花客，绿暗红藏人不识。

留得溪头瑟瑟波，泼成纸上猩猩色。

手把金刀擘彩云，有时剪破秋天碧。

不使红霓段段飞，一时驱上丹霞壁。

蜀客才多染不供，卓文醉后开无力。

孔雀衔来向日飞，翩翩压折黄金翼。

我有歌诗一千首，磨砻山岳罗星斗。

开卷长疑雷电惊，挥毫只怕龙蛇走。

班班布在时人口，满袖松花都未有。

人间无处买烟霞，须知得自神仙手。

也知价重连城璧，一纸万金犹不惜。

薛涛昨夜梦中来，殷勤劝向君边觅。

Song of begging for handcrafted colored note-papers

Wei Zhuang[1]
Tang Dynasty

The glamorous poetess of the Huanhua Stream
secludes herself among dense blooms.
Fetching the upstream crystal-clear water
she douses papers into scarlet red.
Using a golden knife she severs colorful clouds
with scissors to snip off autumn's azure blue.
Rainbows are harnessed before dissipating
into a colorful cliff she forces them to latch onto.
Her paper is not enough for so many talented Shu's
Wenjun is yet to produce more after drinking much wine.
Peacocks holding papers fly toward the sun
their golden wings arching gracefully.
I have penned a thousand song poems
with arrogance dwarfing mountains and engulfing stars.
Lightning crackles when my poem scrolls unfurl
dragons and serpents hide when I lift my brush.
My poems are on everyone's lips
yet not on papers even common as the Pine-Flower.
Nowhere to purchase the misty sunbeams
they are made only by the hands of a celestial.
I know the papers are worth a king's ransom
one piece for ten-thousand of gold I will pay.
Xue Tao emerged in my dream last night
who urged me to ask you for help.

---

1 Wei Zhuang, (c.836−910), courtesy name Duanji, was a native of Jingzhao (now Xi'an, Shaanxi Province). He was the fourth−generation grandson of the poet Wei Yingwu. As a lyricist of the Huajian Faction, his lyrics are elegant and exquisite, with the Huanhua Collection handed down through the generations.

韦庄与浣花溪的缘分始于他担任五代前蜀宰相时，在这里，韦庄写下不少格调新颖、脍炙人口的优秀诗词。《乞彩笺歌》就是其中之一。据传，唐代著名才女薛涛在浣花溪居住时，曾制作精美小彩笺，以笺吟诗。李商隐便有"浣花笺纸桃花色，好好题诗咏玉钩"的赞誉。韦庄此诗更细腻传神地描绘了彩笺的制作精良、色彩明艳、图案生动及价值连城、一纸万金的珍贵，同时，借此彩笺书不朽诗歌，也是这位风雅宰相的美好愿望吧。

The connection between Wei Zhuang and Huanhua Stream dates to the Five Dynasties when he served as prime minister of Qian Shu (907-925), where he wrote many outstanding and popular lyrics in novel style. "Song of Begging for Handcrafted Colored Note-papers" is one of them. It is said that when Xue Tao, a famous talented poetess in the Tang Dynasty lived by Huanhua Stream, once made exquisite small colorful note-papers for poems to be chanted and recorded upon. Li Shangyin also commended them by saying: "peach blossom is the color of the Huanhua Note-papers, compose your poems about the moon more gracefully." In a delicate and expressive way, this poem depicts the note-papers as exquisitely made, with bright colors, vivid patterns and how they are priceless and invaluable. At the same time, it is also this elegant prime minister's good wish to have his monumental poems recorded on the colored note-papers. (By Chen Xin)

唐人韦庄《乞彩笺歌》

浣花溪上如花客，绿闇红藏人
不识。留得溪头瑟瑟波，泼成纸上
猩猩色。手把金刀劈彩云，有时剪
破秋天碧。不使红霓段段飞，一时驱
上丹霞壁。蜀客才多染不供，卓文
醉后开无力。孔雀衔来向日飞翩翩，
历折黄金翼。我有歌诗一千首，磨
砻山岳罗星斗。开卷长疑雷电
惊，挥毫只怕龙蛇走。班班布在时
人口。满袖松花都未有，人间无价
买烟云，须知得向神仙手。也知价
重连城璧，一纸万金犹不惜。薛涛
昨夜梦中来，殷勤劝向君边觅。

唐人韦庄乞彩笺歌
壬寅孟冬 思翔 书于成都

浣花泛舟和韵

〔宋〕吕陶

野店村桥迤逦通，蜀江深处茂林中。

花潭近漾春波绿，彩阁相迎画舫红。

修岸几朝经密雨，芳樽尽日得清风。

诗翁旧隐知何在，且事嬉游与俗同。

Responding to someone's poem from a boat on Huanhua Stream

Lü Tao[1]
Song Dynasty

Village bridges string country stores fore and aft

River Shu meanders through lush deep bamboo groves.

Blossoms dangle above the Ever-blooming Pool's verdant spring ripples,

colorful pavilions greet painted red boats.

The river's embankments serene after showers;

wine is to enjoy all day amid cool breezes.

The great poet once resided somewhere here

let us follow the customs and enjoy this outing.

---

1 Lü Tao (1028–1104), courtesy name Yuan Jun, was a native of Pengshan, Meizhou (in Sichuan Province).

赏析

　　浣花溪，一名濯锦江，又名百花潭，位于四川省成都市西郊，为锦江支流。溪旁有唐代诗人杜甫的故居杜甫草堂、万里桥、青羊宫等名胜，是成都的著名景区。自唐朝以来的一千多年里，以其生态优良、风景优美、人文荟萃而成为游览胜地。蜀人自古有"游乐"之风，宋代文化鼎盛，文士生活悠游，因此浣花溪畔泛舟和文人雅集更是必然。虽然是寻常小诗，但自然环境的旖旎优美、当事人心情的悠然自得，乃至千古名都的从容自信都可以从诗中见其一斑，令千年之后的人们仍陶醉于这村桥茂林、春波画舫、密雨清风的诗意田园。

Appreciation

Huanhua Stream, known as Zhuojin Jiang (Brocade River), was also called Baihua Pool (the Ever-blooming Pool). It is located in the western suburbs of Chengdu City, Sichuan Province as a tributary river of the Brocade River. Along the river, there are scenic spots such as Du Fu's Thatched Cottage (the former residence of Du Fu in the Tang Dynasty), Wanli Bridge, and Qingyang Temple. In the thousand years since the Tang Dynasty, it has become a tourist attraction in Chengdu with its excellent ecology, beautiful scenery, and cultural gatherings. Since ancient times, the people of Shu have had passion for "outings." The literati in the Song Dynasty lived a leisurely life with a thriving culture; boating by the Huanhua Stream and the elegant gatherings were fashionable. Although it is an ordinary poem, the beauty of the natural environment, the leisurely and contented mood of the people on the boat, and even the serenity of the renowned ancient capital city of Chengdu have been vividly depicted. People a thousand years later are still entranced by the picturesque and poetic scenery of villages, bridges, woods, and boats in spring waves, drizzles, and breezes. (By Yang Bei)

唧底柳桥逦迤

通昌江深雷戍

塔中古塔浮画

漾春波添孙写

枕迎画船孤修

客几和堆要为

芳指杏日满清风

韵翁焦隐知何

在此了塘村与佳

月

幽兰浣花沿丹和韵

壬寅初夏

思中书

和子由《蚕市》

〔宋〕苏轼

蜀人衣食常苦艰，蜀人游乐不知还。

千人耕种万人食，一年辛苦一春闲。

闲时尚以蚕为市，共忘辛苦逐欣欢。

去年霜降斫秋荻，今年箔积如连山。

破瓢为轮土为釜，争买不翅金与纨。

忆昔与子皆童卯，年年废书走市观。

市人争夸斗巧智，野人喑哑遭欺谩。

诗来使我感旧事，不悲去国悲流年。

In response to Ziyou's poem about "Silk Festival"

Su Shi[1]
Song Dynasty

The lives of the Shu are hard,

but they also indulge in outings and pleasure-seeking.

One needs to toil to feed ten mouths and

spring is the only time for leisure throughout the year.

That is when people celebrate silk festivals,

and flock together to leave their hardships behind.

Autumn reeds were harvested under frost the year before;

they stretch into mountains of cocoon bedding this year.

The silk reeling instruments are merely gourds or earthen wares,

yet they are hot sellers equal to gold and white silk.

I recall when we were both adolescents,

we would play hooky to attend silk festivals.

Folks would try to outsmart one another at bargaining;

those slow with words were always the losing ones.

Your poem brought back all these past memories;

I lament not being away, but how time flies!

---

1 Su Shi (1037−1101), courtesy name Zizhan, also known as "a lay Buddhist from Dongpo", was a native of Meishan, Meizhou (now Meishan in Sichuan Province). Su Shi was a literary leader in mid-Northern Song Dynasty who exceled in poetry, *ci*, prose, calligraphy and painting. His poems cover a variety of subjects using exaggerations and metaphors with a unique style.

传说成都自蚕丛开国教民农桑，就有了悠久的蚕桑种植和"蚕市"历史。"蚕市"既是桑蚕农事交易市场，也有游玩赏乐性质，商贾云集生意买卖之外，更有呼朋唤友游玩、观光、饮酒、娱乐。至宋代，蚕市已成为重要的节庆游乐活动。苏轼虽出生于川蜀，但与弟弟苏辙长期为官外地。一次，苏辙将一首回忆家乡蚕市的诗寄给哥哥，瞬间便触动了诗人的乡愁。诗人神游儿时故乡，不禁思绪联翩，故作此和诗。诗中追忆当年与弟弟一起逃学游观蚕市，蚕市熙熙攘攘，桑民斗智争巧。诗句满载着对家乡人情风土的深深眷恋，也流露出离家远宦、逝水流年的人生感叹。

It is said that since Cancong founded the ancient kingdom of Shu, he taught his people to breed silkworms and grow mulberry. There has been a long history of sericulture and silkworm markets in Chengdu. The Silk Festival was not only for mulberry and silkworm-related business, but also a time for enjoyment. In addition to silk business, crowded merchants also invited friends to play, enjoy sightseeing, drink rice wine, and seek entertainment there. By the Song Dynasty, the market had become an important festival and place of entertainment. Although Su Shi was born in Sichuan, he and his younger brother Su Zhe had been officials outside of Sichuan for a long time. Su Zhe once sent a poem to his brother, recalling the silk festivals in their hometown, which instantly evoked the poet's nostalgia for home. His mind couldn't stop wandering when recalling his hometown in his childhood. He responded with this poem full of fond childhood memories and idyllic hometown customs. The poem recalled the time when he and his younger brother played truant and went to the silk festivals. It depicts memories of the bustling festival-like market with sericulture farmers bargaining out of their wits. It is full of sentimental longing for the customs of their hometown as well as the poet's lamentation for the passing of time and being an official far away from home. (By Yang Bei)

蜀人衣食常苦艰，蜀人游乐不知还。

千人耕种万人食，一年辛苦一春闲。

闲时尚以蚕为市，共忘辛苦逐欣欢。

去年霜降斫秋获，今年陆杷少连山破。

筲积少连山破，瓢罂散金钱为釜。

争买不如金，忆昔曾与子皆。

童稚年年旷书，走市觐市人争。

诱斗巧智野人，暗哑遭毁诟诗。

来使我感焦然，事不忘故国情。

流年

苏轼和子由蚕市　壬寅端午果林书

夜闻浣花江声甚壮

〔宋〕陆游

浣花之东当笮桥，奔流啮桥桥为摇。

分洪初疑两蛟舞，触石散作千珠跳。

壮声每挟雷雨横，巨势潜借鼋鼍骄。

梦回闻之坐太息，铁衣何日东征辽？

衔枚度碛沙飒飒，盘槊断陇风萧萧。

不然投檄径归去，短篷卧听钱塘潮。

On hearing the mighty
Huanhua Stream torrent at night

Lu You[1]
Song Dynasty

A bamboo bridge stretches east on Huanhua Stream,

rocking in the swift pounding torrent.

Diverging currents dance as two river dragons,

their waves crashing into thousands of drops.

The roaring river rushes as a thunderous storm,

as if giant tortoises and crocodiles stir colossal waves.

Awakened from a dream of raging waters, I sit and sigh;

when will I armor up against the Jerchens in the east again?

When sands shifted as soldiers march silently through the desert;

winds howled as we brandished spears against charging enemies.

Why not just resign from officialdom and return home,

Rest in a boat and listen to the Qiantang tidal bore.

1　Lu You (1125−1210) was a prominent patriotic poet of the Southern Song Dynasty, whose poems are
unrestrained and bold, full of fighting spirit and nationalistic passions.

此诗写于陆游寓居成都时期。诗开篇不凡，前六句以想象、夸张手法描绘夏季浣花溪奔腾汹涌、水流湍急、惊涛拍岸的壮观景色，引发诗人梦回曾经的驰骋疆场、铁马冰河。后六句笔锋一转，追忆往昔衔枚度碛、盘槊断陇的峥嵘岁月，绘画出征战的残酷与艰难。然而更为感慨的是诗人壮士扼腕、报国无门、有心杀敌、无力回天的命运悲剧。

南宋偏安苟且的屈辱中，一位文则诗名满天下、武则挺剑刺乳虎的英雄，最终却只能"投檄径归去，短篷卧听钱塘潮"，成为那个悲情时代的注脚。

This poem was written during Lu You's tenure in Chengdu with an extraordinary opening. Through visualization and exaggeration, the first six lines portray a magnificent view of Huanhua Stream in summer with surging rapids, rushing torrents, thunderous roars and colossal waves crashing onto embankments. The scene triggers the poet's memories of riding his armored horse over frozen rivers and through battlefields. The following six lines switch over to the memorable years of marching through deserts discretely and banishing his spear at the charging enemies. The verses paint the cruelty and hardships of war expeditions. The most difficult for the poet was the lack of ways to serve the country, leading to a tragic life with no place to put in use his true prowess.

Thus, in the weak Southern Song Dynasty content with only partial sovereignty, this gifted heroic poet with superb military feats can't help but lament in the end: "Why not just resign from officialdom and return home, to rest in a boat and listen to the Qiantang tidal bore." (By Zhou Yiqiao)

浣花之東當筍
橋畣流啮橋橋
為粮分洪初疑兩
蛟舞觸石散作
千珠跳抃聲每
挾雷雨橫兵勢
潛借電黿竈驕夢
回閭之坒太息鐵
衣何日東征遼衛
枚度磧沙颯
盤興節隴風蕭
不然投檄徑歸
去短蓬遲臥飛錢
塘潮
陸游夜聞浣花江
聲甚壯
壬寅端午思齊書

青羊宫小饮赠道士

〔宋〕陆游

青羊道士竹为家，也种玄都观里花。

微雨晴时看鹤舞，小窗幽处听蜂衙。

药垆宿火荧荧暖，醉袖迎风猎猎斜。

老我一官真漫浪，会来分子淡生涯。

To the Daoist priest of the Qingyang Temple after tea

Lu You
Song Dynasty

Daoist priests of Qingyang reside among bamboo,

peach blossoms of the Xuandu Temple are also abundant here.

Cranes dance in the distant mist after drizzle,

as bees hum music by the side window.

A medicine pot is kept warm on an overnight stove;

head-on breezes flutter my sleeves as I tipsily stroll.

A carefree officer at my old age,

happy to chat about a life without fame and success.

青羊宫被誉为"川西第一道观"，传说为神仙聚会、老子传道的圣地。诗歌作于陆游在青羊宫旁浣花溪畔的闲居时期。与其前期诗歌不同，此诗俨然一派安闲自在之趣。竹林苍翠，微雨轩窗，看花开鹤舞，任暖荧醉袖。似不问世事，超脱尘俗。但对闲适生活的细腻描写中，隐藏着诗人极其矛盾的内心世界，渴望兼济天下的政治抱负与期盼独善其身的士人情致一直纠缠于生命深处，现实生活中无法实现的壮志豪情只能委曲婉转于退隐中的闲情逸趣，希冀在"山重水复"之中开拓出一片"柳暗花明"。

Qingyang Temple has been known as the most prominent Daoist temple in western Sichuan. Legend has it that the immortals used to gather there, and Laozi, the founder of Daoism, elucidated on his teachings at that spot. Lu You penned this poem when he was residing near Huanghua Stream by Qingyang Temple. Different from his previous poems, he sounded aloof and at ease in this one. The poet admired lush green bamboo groves, the drizzle outside wooden windows, cranes dancing among blossoms, and the warm fire in the stove as he tipsily staggered along. Though seemingly immersed in seclusion and out of the mundane world, through delicate description of his life in leisure, the poet's extremely contradictory inner world is revealed. Deep in his heart, the political yearning to serve the country as an elite, and the scholarly call to focus on self-virtue, mix and intertwine. The unachievable lofty goals and ambitions in real life needed to give way to leisure and joy in his retreat. However, there is still hope that "after endless mountains and rivers," "bright flowers" will emerge eventually beyond "the shade of a willow." (By Zhou Yiqiao)

青羊道士竹

吾家世種玄

都觀里花微

兩晴時看鷺

舞山漁樵靄

聽蜂衛葉鑑

宿火荧荧暖醉

袖迎風獵獵斜

老我一官真漫

浪會來分予子

浮生涯

陸游青羊宮

小欲贈道士

壬寅端午後一日

田雪平書於成都

锦城竹枝词

〔清〕 杨燮

川人终是爱高腔，几部丝弦住老郎。

彩凤不输陈四喜，泰洪班里黑娃强。

只说高腔有苟莲，万头攒看万家传。

生夸彭四旦双彩，可惜斯文张四贤。

清唱洋琴赛出名，新年杂耍遍蓉城。

淮书一阵莲花落，都爱廖儿哭五更。

玉泰班中薛打鼓，滚珠洒豆妙难言。

少年健羡多花点，学向元宵打十番。

无数伶人东角住，顺城房屋长丁男。

五童神庙天涯石，一路芳邻近魏三。

迎晖门内土牛过，旌旆飞扬笑语和。

人似山来春似海，高妆女戏踏空过。

Bamboo songs of the Brocade City

Yang Xie[1]
Qing Dynasty

Sichuan folks love their high-pitched opera the most;

many are performed at the Laolang Temple.

Cai Feng enjoys the same popularity as Chen Sixi;

Hei Wa is the lead for the Taihong Troupe.

For high-pitched singers, Gou Lian is number one;

many flock to see the talents of the Wans.

Peng Si for the male lead and Shuang Cai the female lead,

both shine over the more refined Zhang Sixian.

For solos you go to the dulcimer competitions,

variety shows throughout the City of Hibiscus in the New Year.

There is also the Huai style storytelling of the Lotus Flower rhyme,

all loved to watch Liao'er "Wailing at Dawn".

Xue masters his drumbeats in Yutai Troupe,

memorizing their sounds as rolling beads and scattering beans.

Many a young lad takes to the fancy beats,

during the lantern festival they try out the Shifan.

Numerous performers reside by the southeast corner,

and so the households of Shuncheng expands.

Along the streets of Wutong Temple and Tianya Boulder,

folks cluster near the respected master Wei San.

A mud buffalo is carried past the East Gate,

as flags and pennants flutter over happy bustling masses.

Large crowds gather amid peak spring hues,

as women on stilts tiptoe over peoples' heads.

1　Yang Xie, courtesy name Duishan, was a famous poet in the Qing Dynasty. He was a native in Chengdu and a successful candidate in the imperial examinations at the provincial level in the sixth year of the Qing Dynasty Jiaqing Reign.

生旦净末丑，演绎人间百态；昆高胡弹灯，唱尽人生百味。深受巴蜀人民喜爱的川剧艺术，博采众家，源远流长，在中国戏曲史及巴蜀文化发展史上具有十分独特的地位，位列我国首批国家级非物质文化遗产名录，是川渝文化艺术中一张璀璨的名片。成都自古就有"蜀戏冠天下"的美誉，川剧历代兴盛，具有厚重鲜明的天府文化特点。此诗为清代诗人杨燮《锦城竹枝词百首》其中六首。"川人终是爱高腔"，六首诗生动描绘了当时川剧精湛的表演技艺及人们趋之若鹜的情形，展示了当时成都及巴蜀地区川剧的演出盛况。

The young male leads, the female leads, the painted, the old male leads, and the jesters all interpret and mimic aspects of human lives. The Kun style, the high-pitched Chuan, the two-stringed Huqin, the Qin style, and the lantern operas touch upon all flavors of life. Much loved by the people of Ba-Shu, the art of Sichuan Opera has a long history. It shares aspects of many other operas and occupies a unique place in the history of Chinese operas and the cultural development history of Ba-Shu. It is one of China's first examples of intangible cultural heritage and a dazzling representation of Sichuan and Chongqing cultural art. Since ancient times, Chengdu has boasted of its opera as among the best in the world. Sichuan operas, long or short, have flourished over the ages, representing the characteristics of the proper and distinctive Tianfu culture. This collection of six short pieces is from the "One Hundred Bamboo Songs of the Brocade City" written by Yang Xie, a poet of the Qing Dynasty. "The Chuan folks love their high-pitched opera the most," the six poems vividly depict the exquisite performing talents of Sichuan opera and the audience drawn to them, showing the spectacular nature of Sichuan opera in Chengdu and the Ba-Shu region at that time. (By Liu Ying)

川人終是愛高
腔幾部絲絲弦
伴老郎彩鳳
不輸陳四喜泰
洪璉裹黑娃孫
只說高腔有苟
蓮萬頭攢看
萬家傳生誇
彭四旦雙彩可
惜斯文張四顯
清唱洋琴賽出
名新年雜耍
遍蕓城淮書一
陳蓮花落都
愛摩兒哭五更
玉泰班中薛

打鼓滾珠洒
豈妙雜言少年
健兒多花難掌
向元宵打十番
喜鼓修人東角
住順城房屋長
丁男五壹神廟
天涯石一路芳鄰
近魏三迎暉門
內土牛過旌旆
飛揚笑語和人
似山來春似海
高妝女戲蹻空
過
揚蔓錦城竹枝詞
壬辰游夏田翠書

070

花会场竹枝词

〔清〕 谢家驹

二月花朝雨后晴，

锦官城外荡舟行。

红颜却怕红尘染，

不听人声听水声。

A bamboo song from the Flower Festival

Xie Jiaju[1]
Qing Dynasty

Rain breaks for the Flower Festival of the second lunar moon,

as boats row about outside the Brocade City.

A beauty enjoys serenity away from the mundane world,

the sound of water more alluring than bustling masses.

---

1   Xie Jiaju, courtesy name Longwen, also known as Xia Sheng, was born in late Qing Dynasty. He was a
native of Nanchuan, Sichuan provice (Today's Nanchuan District, Chongqing City).

花朝节，指孟春之时人们为百花庆祝生日的节日，简称花朝。成都花朝节历史悠久，最早可追溯到西汉，距今已有一千多年。蜀人尚游玩，每当春和景明、姹紫嫣红的花朝时节，便竞相外出，踏春、赏花、划船、戏水，载歌载舞，欢声笑语，体现了人们对美好生活极其浪漫的追求与向往。此诗描写了一次花朝中，诗人在锦江中荡舟游乐时的惬意与欢欣，同时也在动静相宜处描绘了清幽婉转的水声。而"红颜却怕红尘染，不听人声听水声"一句意味深长，以"香草美人"手法含蓄表达了自己洁身自爱、清雅高洁的情怀，蕴藉着于外在喧哗躁动之中坚守内心的品格追求。

Appreciation

The Flower Festival, known as Huazhao, is a festival during which people celebrate all the blossoms in the spring. The Chengdu Flower Festival has a long history, tracing back to the Western Han Dynasty more than a thousand years ago. During the bright and colorful Flower Festival every spring, Shu people flocked to the suburbs on spring outings to enjoy blooming flowers, boating, playing in the water, singing, and dancing with hearty chatter and laughter. The festival is symbolic of the romantic pursuits and yearning for a better life. This poem depicts the poet's coziness and joy when boating on the Brocade River during the Flower Festival, as well as the subtle sound of still water juxtaposed with the clamor and bustle on shore. The phrase "a beauty enjoys serenity away from the mundane world, the sound of water more alluring than bustling masses" is a meaningful expression. By expressing "a beauty and sweet sage," the poet subtly expressed his aspiration to remain untainted, aloof, and elegant. It implies the poet's pursuit to maintain faith within noisy and restless surroundings. (By Liu Ying)

二月花朝雨後
晴錦官城外
蕩舟行紅顏
却怕紅塵染
不聽人聲聒
水聲

謝家駒花會場
竹枝詞
壬寅瑞陽之節
昂平壽萩錦城

丈人山

〔唐〕杜甫

自为青城客，不唾青城地。

为爱丈人山，丹梯近幽意。

丈人祠西佳气浓，缘云拟住最高峰。

扫除白发黄精在，君看他时冰雪容。

Mount Elder (Mount Qingcheng)

Du Fu
Tang Dynasty

As a dweller upon Mount Qingcheng,

 I take care not to spit on its ground.

How I love Mount Elder,

 its skyward steps leading to tranquil serenity.

West of the Mount Elder Temple is most appealing;

 I wish to drift on clouds to reside on its tallest pcak.

My grey hair will surely be reversed by its elixir,

 and radiate youth and vigor when you see me again.

自古诗人皆入蜀，入蜀皆游青城山。自古以来，有关青城山的经典之作不胜枚举，其中杜甫的《丈人山》堪称佳作。丈人山，即青城山，在青城县西北三十二里处，传说能积火自焚、随烟气上下的神人宁封曾诗意地栖居于此，后来黄帝筑坛，拜他为师，尊称其为"五岳丈人"，青城山也因此有了"丈人山"的美誉。丹梯千级，迤逦而上。一路走过，穿林而来的山风，流洗碎石的清泉，无不让诗人尽感清远幽深之意。丈人祠西升腾卷舒的云雾缥缈脱俗，即使诗圣也不免萌生求仙成道之愿。杜甫以"青城客"自喻，表达出对青城山的无限热爱。如今，《丈人山》一诗刻于青城山天师洞的石壁处，更为这一灵山圣地添染了无限诗意。

Appreciation

Shu has drawn poets since ancient times, with Mount Qingcheng as a must-visit location. There is a long list of classic poems about Mount Qingcheng, among which Du Fu's "Mount Elder" is of particular note. Mount Elder (Mount Qingcheng) lies thirty-two *li* northwest of the Qingcheng County. Legend has it that it had the capability of self-immolation. Ning Feng, an immortal who ascends and descends through smoke, is depicted in poems as a poetic inhabitant of Mount Qingcheng. The Yellow Emperor constructed an altar to recognize Ning Feng as a master teacher and honored him "the Elder of the Five Sacred Mountains," leading to Mount Qingcheng's alternate name, "Mount Elder." Du Fu depicts the countless steps winding their way to the top of the mountain; mountain breezes blowing through the forests and crystal springs add to the tranquility and serenity. The clouds and mist rising in the winds west of the Temple of Mount Elder are so ethereal that even the sage poet can not help but wish to become immortal. Du Fu calls himself dweller of Mount Qingcheng, which demonstrates his infinite love for the mountain. Today, the poem is engraved on the stone wall of the Tian Shi Cave on Mount Qingcheng, adding to the poetic nature of the sacred holy mountain. (By Niu Xiaodan)

自古青城多不
唾青城地為愛
文人山丹梯近
此意文人祠在
佳氣氲綠
雲擬住家高峰
掃除白髮黃精
在君看他時冰
雪客
梵音文人山
壬寅端午後一日
思平書於成都

到蜀后记途中经历

〔唐〕雍陶

剑峰重叠雪云漫，忆昨来时处处难。

大散岭头春足雨，褒斜谷里夏犹寒。

蜀门去国三千里，巴路登山八十盘。

自到成都烧酒熟，不思身更入长安。

Recalling the journey along
the way after arriving in Shu

Yong Tao[1]
Tang Dynasty

Cloud-wrapped jagged snow peaks one after another

every step an arduous undertaking as I recall.

Incessant spring drizzles on Dasan Hill

summer in Baoxie Valley chilly still.

Shu Kingdom is three thousand *li* away from the capital

the Ba Mountain path winds through eighty turns.

Distillation ready to savor after reaching Chengdu

I will forget about returning to my officialdom in Chang'an.

---

1   Born in Chengdu, Yong Tao (c. 789−c. 873), courtesy name Guo Jun, was a poet in late Tang Dynasty. Although he lived in poverty when he was young, he worked hard. In 834, he became a successful candidate in the highest imperial examinations and was endorsed by most celebrities at that time, which paved the way for his official career.

蜀道艰难，剑阁峥嵘，一夫当关，万夫莫开。难怪诗仙李白高呼"蜀道之难，难于上青天"。雍陶的这首诗以回忆手法记述入蜀途中高山深谷的艰险历程，亦深寓诗人身世经历的艰难险阻和对宦途生活的厌倦。开篇点题，剑阁崔嵬，百步九折，积雪皑皑，绵延不断。颔联写春雨飘洒，泥泞难行；山高水险，夏日清寒。颈联扣"远""曲"二字，写京、蜀二地，遥遥三千里；回旋曲折，足足八十盘。心惊魄动，抚膺长叹。末联收束，回顾羁旅行程，感慨仕途艰难，而成都美食美酒令人留恋，足以乐不思归。诗句或为调侃，但诗人倦于利禄奔走淡泊宦情，且把锦城作故园的心情或许也并不是虚妄之言。

Treacherous is the Shu Pass, rugged and steep, the fort of Jiange: "A single guard on the pass, and a force ten-thousand strong laments." No wonder Li Bai, the poet of celestial talent exclaimed: "It would be easier to reach the azure sky than climbing the Shu pass!" This poem by Yong Tao is an account recollecting the treacherous journey through jagged mountains and deep ravines to Shu, paralleling the hardships of the author's personal life as well as weariness of his former official life. The opening line describes the road through Jiange as rugged and treacherous, full of twists and turns, stretching along under snow cover. The second line references how the spring rain made the roads muddy and even more difficult to traverse, while tall peaks and turbulent rapids made the summer chilly. The third line is closely focused on the words "far" and "torturous." The distant 3,000 *li* path from the capital to Sichuan is described as frightening and heart-pounding, as it twists and turns a full eighty times. The last line recalls the trip and laments the difficulties of the author's career, tempered by wine and savory cuisine seductive enough to keep people in Chengdu. The verses are perhaps just the poet's ridicule, but the author's weariness of fortune and officialdom as well as his willingness to make Chengdu his hometown may not simply be in jest. (By Niu Xiaodan)

剑峰重叠白云堆

云漫怆眼来

时雪继大散

岭头春足雨襄

斜谷栈里夏犹寒

蜀门去国三千里

巴路登山八十盤

自到成都饶酒

熟不思身更入

长安

龙陶到蜀渡记

途中经历

壬寅距芒种雨日

思知中书于成都

鹊桥仙·乘槎归去

〔宋〕苏轼

乘槎归去，成都何在，万里江沱汉漾。

与君各赋一篇诗，留织女、鸳鸯机上。

还将旧曲，重赓新韵，须信吾侪天放。

人生何处不儿嬉，看乞巧、朱楼彩舫。

To the tune of Reunion on the Magpie Bridge-Boarding a bamboo raft on return (Responding to Su Jian's poem on Chinese Valentine's Day)

Su Shi
Song Dynasty

Boarding a bamboo raft on return

which direction is Chengdu?

The mighty rivers of Han and Tuo endlessly flow.

We each crafted a poem

about the legend of the weaver girl, with

her brocade weaving loom.

Let me edit my poem from the past and

Recraft it to the tune of your poem

as we are both free and unconstrained.

Life is like a child's play throughout

as in praying for wisdom on Chinese Valentine's

some trying their luck on verandas, others on painted boats.

苏轼只有青年时期与成都有几次交集，但苏轼的成都情结却贯穿其一生。创作这首词时，诗人任杭州知州，七夕之夜，与苏坚诗词唱和，由鸳鸯织机、巧女织锦联想到家乡锦城、亲人相知。当年 20 岁的苏轼辞家远行，踏上波诡云谲的仕途之旅，便再也没有回去。此去经年，山高水长，人生漂泊，乡关难忘。万里江汉滔滔逝，乘槎归去梦故乡，词里有一代文豪对家乡的深切眷恋，也有旷达超然、随性豁达的生命体验。大江东去浪淘尽，千古风流日月长。东坡路、苏坡路、东坡街道、东坡大道、东坡公园、东坡小学、东坡雕塑、三苏浮雕……斯人已去，但这些命名中，依稀可以见词人斑斓人生中留于家乡的雪泥鸿爪。

There have been only a few interactions between Su Shi and Chengdu during his youth. However, Su Shi's attachment to Chengdu continued throughout his life. Su Shi was the prefect of Hangzhou when he composed this poem. On the night of *Qixi* (Chinese Valentine's Day), he and Su Jian, his brother, responded to each other's poems. The twin looms and weaver girls fabricating brocades reminded them of their hometown, the Brocade City, and their relatives there. At the age of 20, Su Shi set off from his home to embark on a precarious career and never returned. Though years went by, blocked by tall mountains and meandering rivers, the vagrant wanderer could not forget his hometown: "The mighty River Han endlessly flows, a bamboo raft carries me to the homeland in dreams." The lyric contains the eminent poet's deep love for his hometown, as well as his free and open-minded attitude towards life: "The mighty river easterly flows with waves lashing on, gone are all the great men who shine in history." Dongpo Road, Supo Road, Dongpo Street, Dongpo Avenue, Dongpo Park, Dongpo Primary School, Dongpo Sculpture, the carvings of the three Su's… Though all bygone, through these names, we can still detect traces of legacy the author left behind for his hometown during his colorful career. (By Niu Xiaodan)

乘槎歸去成 莫何在萬里

江沱漢漾与

君亏賦一篇詩

留織女駕雙機

上遲將舊曲

重廣新韻須

信吾倚天放

人生何需不覺

嬉看乞巧朱

樓彩舫

蘇軾鵲橋仙
乘槎歸去
壬寅芒種日
昭平書

题黄筌芙蓉图

〔宋〕赵构

照水枝枝蜀锦囊,

年年泽国为谁芳?

朱颜自得西风意,

不管千林一夜霜。

Responding to Huang Quan's beautiful painting of hibiscus

Zhao Gou[1]
Song Dynasty

Shu brocade pouches hang on waterside branches,

for whom do they blossom year after year?

As if a westerly breeze intensifies their vibrant hues,

they still shine among a thousand frostbitten twigs.

---

1 Zhao Gou (1107−1187), courtesy name Deji, was the founding emperor of the Southern Song Dynasty. He wrote this poem praising the painting of hibiscus flowers by the famous painter Huang Quan of west Sichuan during the Five Dynasties. Painting inscriptions was a refined art popular among Chinese poets, especially in Song Dynasty. It artistically combined Chinese poetry, calligraphy and painting, which complemented one another in form. This not only sublimated the beauty of poetry and painting, but also extended the artistic imagery.

题画向来为中国诗人雅事，宋朝尤为盛行，是中国诗、书、画三者在形式上相得益彰的艺术沟通。它不仅增加了诗画的美感，也丰富了其意境。

芙蓉自古以来深受蜀地人民的喜爱，后蜀皇帝曾命百姓在城墙上遍植芙蓉，"每至秋，四十里锦绣"，故成都号称"蓉城"。如今成都大街小巷芙蓉摇曳，花开时节，锦城红遍，更在1983年被正式确定为成都市市花。宋代帝王多才艺，以画为诗，不仅描绘出芙蓉照水的娇艳姿态，更赞美它在深秋绽放不惧霜侵露凌的高洁精神。意境的升华赋予了芙蓉以不俗的人格："你是端庄美丽的"。

Painting inscriptions was a refined art popular among Chinese poets, especially in Song Dynasty. It artistically combined Chinese poetry, calligraphy, and painting, which complemented one another in form. This not only sublimated the beauty of poetry and painting, but also extended the artistic imagery.

People of the Shu region have long adored hibiscus flowers since ancient times. The Emperor of Later Shu once ordered people to plant hibiscus on the city walls. As every fall, hibiscus blooms stretch forty *li* along the walls, Chengdu is hence known as "Rong Cheng," or the City of Hibiscus. Nowadays, hibiscuses dangle all over streets and alleys of Chengdu. The entire city is dotted with bright crimson when they blossom. In 1983, hibiscus was officially designated as the city flower of Chengdu. Zhao Gou, the versatile emperor of the Song Dynasty, combined poetry and painting to not only depict the delicate and beautiful posture of the hibiscus reflected in water, but also to highlight the unyielding, noble spirit of the flower that chose to bloom in chilly late autumn. Through these artistic depictions, the hibiscus took on an elegant personality of dignity and charm. (By Guo Lili)

照水枝：蜀錦

囊羞：澤國

為誰芳朱顏

自渭西風意不

管千林一夜霜

趙構題黃筌芙蓉圖

壬寅芒種日

田蘊章書於成都

蔬食戏书

〔宋〕陆游

新津韭黄天下无，色如鹅黄三尺余。

东门彘肉更奇绝，肥美不减胡羊酥。

贵珍讵敢杂常馔，桂炊薏米圆比珠。

还吴此味那复有，日饭脱粟焚枯鱼。

人生口腹何足道，往往坐役七尺躯。

膻荤从今一扫除，夜煮白石笺阴符。

Ribbing at my vegetarian diet

Lu You
Song Dynasty

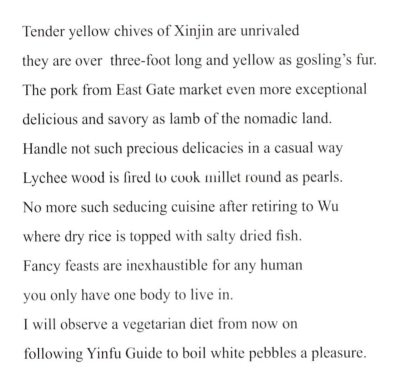

Tender yellow chives of Xinjin are unrivaled

they are over three-foot long and yellow as gosling's fur.

The pork from East Gate market even more exceptional

delicious and savory as lamb of the nomadic land.

Handle not such precious delicacies in a casual way

Lychee wood is fired to cook millet round as pearls.

No more such seducing cuisine after retiring to Wu

where dry rice is topped with salty dried fish.

Fancy feasts are inexhaustible for any human

you only have one body to live in.

I will observe a vegetarian diet from now on

following Yinfu Guide to boil white pebbles a pleasure.

陆游在蜀中生活不满七年，但却留下了上千篇作品，留下了对成都刻骨铭心的喜爱与思念，离开成都后又写下为数不少的忆蜀思蜀之作，甚至将自己的诗集命名为《剑南诗稿》。"老子从来薄宦情，不辞落魄锦官城"，对成都的偏爱溢于言表。

这首七言歌行便是回忆当年成都美食之作。天府之国物产丰饶，美食之盛自然也是诗人"成都情结"之一，"风雨春残杜鹃笑，夜夜寒食梦还蜀""东来坐阁七寒暑，未尝举箸忘吾蜀"……东归七年之后，每当举起筷子之时，仍会想起"吾蜀"——成都，他难以忘怀的"第二故乡"。

Lu You lived in Chengdu for no more than seven years, but left behind more than a thousand poems embedded with an unforgettable love and longing for the city. Even after leaving Chengdu, he wrote a substantial number of works recalling the city, and named his own collection of poems "A Collection of Poems from Jiannan (Chengdu)." The poet never minced his praise for Chengdu, such as "I've never cared about being an official, content I am to be a nobody just in the Brocade City."

This seven-character poem is to recall Chengdu's cuisine of the time. As a land of abundance, Chengdu boasts a thousand *li* of fertile fields with abundant produce. The rich cuisine naturally added to the poet's love for Chengdu: "Rain and wind signal late spring but azaleas shine, on every chilly night I dream of returning to Shu." In another, he writes: "It's been seven winters and summers since returning east; I've not forgotten about Shu whenever picking up chopsticks." Seven years after returning to the east, whenever he raises his chopsticks, he misses Chengdu— "my beloved Chengdu", his unforgettable "second hometown." (By Yang Xi)

新津韭黃天下無色如鵝黃三尺餘東門彘肉更奇絶肥美不減胡羊酥貴詎敢雜常饌桂炊薏米圓比珠還吳此味邪得意日飯脫粟樊枯魚人生口腹何足道徒坐役七尺軀膻葷泥今一掃除夜煮白石餐陰荷

陸游蔬食戲書

多字芒種後一日

思翁書於成都

怀锦水居止 · 其二

〔唐〕杜甫

万里桥南宅，百花潭北庄。

层轩皆面水，老树饱经霜。

雪岭界天白，锦城曛日黄。

惜哉形胜地，回首一茫茫！

Recollecting my cottage
by the Brocade Water– No.2

Du Fu
Tang Dynasty

My cottage is west of the Wanli Bridge,

and north of the Ever-blooming Pool.

Wooden grid windows overlook water,

with weather-beaten trees aging beyond.

Snowy peaks merge with the shining bright sky,

the Brocade City dons a sunset yellow.

Alas my splendid hometown,

in a vast haze of memory.

杜甫"五载客蜀郡，一年居梓州"，从759年入蜀到765年离开，杜甫结庐浣花溪畔，虽然生活拮据，但成都的闲适和温润滋养了这位漂泊者的心。这首诗作于765年秋。因战乱，杜甫全家再次离开浣花溪草堂，乘舟东下来到云安（今四川云阳）。而这最后一次在云安的怀念，又比前几次的怀念深刻得多。诗人似乎预感到战乱背景下唐朝江河日下的颓败之势，成都虽蜀中"形胜之地"，亦同样前途茫茫。回首昔日桥下江云远眺，花溪竹林醉卧，不禁怅然。诗中对草堂的怀念，不仅是对个人"居止"的依依眷恋，同时也是对成都的由衷爱恋，甚或也是诗圣对曾经的开元盛世人民安定、国家安宁的难以泯灭的留恋。

From his arrival in Shu in 759 to his departure in 765, Du Fu "dwelled five years in the prefecture of Shu, with one more year in Zizhou." Du Fu built his cottage by Huanhua Stream. Although he had a meager living, Chengdu's leisure and warmth nourished the wanderer's heart. This poem was written in the autumn of 765. Due to the turmoil of war, Du's family left the thatched cottage once more, sailed east by boat, and arrived in Yun'an (now Yunyang, Sichuan). His last recollection of his cottage after arriving in Yun'an carries a much more profound connotation than the previous ones. The poet seemed to have a premonition of the Tang Empire's rapid decline against the background of the raging war. Though known as the "blessed land of Shu," his vision of Chengdu's future was nevertheless bleak. The poet could not help but feel despondent when he recalled how in bygone days, he gazed afar at the clouds over the river and tipsily relaxed in bamboo grooves by the floral stream. Thus, the sage poet's yearning for the thatched cottage in the poem is not only a lingering attachment to his personal dwelling, but also his heartfelt love for Chengdu and an indelible nostalgia for the bygone peace and stability of the people and state during the Flourishing Age of Kaiyuan. (By Zhu Ling)

第五橋南宅
百花潭北莊
層軒皆面水
老樹飽經霜
雪嶺界天白
錦城曛日黃
惜哉形勝地
回首一茫茫

杜甫懷錦水居止
壬寅冬　思邦書

杜鹃城
（dù juān chéng）

〔清〕卫道凝
（qīng）（wèi dào níng）

沃野蚕丛国，城荒杜宇基。
（wò yě cán cóng guó）（chéng huāng dù yǔ jī）

井梧春蘸雨，原柳晚垂丝。
（jǐng wú chūn zhàn yǔ）（yuán liǔ wǎn chuí sī）

家解粳炊玉，人知竹酿醾。
（jiā jiě jīng chuī yù）（rén zhī zhú niàng mí）

年年寒食节，清夜子规啼。
（nián nián hán shí jié）（qīng yè zǐ guī tí）

The Cuckoo City

Wei Daoning[1]
Qing Dynasty

On the fertile land of the Silkworm God,

ancient King Duyu's palace lies in ruins.

Well-side parasol trees damp after drizzle,

willows droop on the plain at dusk.

Jade-like white rice is steamed by all households,

as favored wine brews in bamboo containers.

During the Cold Food Festival,

cuckoos' calls echo deep into the evening.

1　Wei Daoning (1762−1823), courtesy name Huan Zhi, was a literatus of the Qing Dynasty and a native of Pi County, Chengdu.

卫道凝为清朝文人，他在本诗中写了他的家乡郫县——今成都市郫都区的历史风貌。郫都区位于成都市西北部近郊，在秦灭蜀后始称为郫县。2016年，成都市正式撤销郫县，设立成都市郫都区。

郫县历史悠久，自古不凡。古蜀国国王杜宇曾定都于郫，相传他在国亡身死后化作杜鹃鸟，故古时郫县别名"杜鹃城"。古蜀国沃野千里，从首位国王蚕丛起，代代励精图治，尤其传至杜宇，迁都郫邑，教民耕种，开疆拓土，处处春烟杨柳，家家玉食美酒。后禅位于同姓族人杜灵，自己修道，死后化为杜鹃鸟，即诗中的"子规"，声声啼血，思念故国。

Wei Daoning was a literatus of the Qing Dynasty. This poem describes the historical and cultural background of his hometown, Pi County, today's Pidu District, Chengdu. Pidu District, located in the northwestern suburbs of Chengdu, was called Pi County after Qin conquered Shu, until 2016 when Chengdu officially renamed it the "Pidu District" of Chengdu. Pi County, well-known since ancient times, has a long history. Du Yu, the king of the ancient Shu Kingdom, chose to build his capital in Pi.

Ancient Shu was fertile and prosperous and every king since the first King of Shu, the Silkworm God (Can Cong) was diligent in their reigns. During Du Yu's reign, he moved the capital to Pi, taught people to farm, expanded the territory, and turned the area into a land of abundance with delicate food, delicious wine, and misty spring willows. After Du Yu abdicated and handed over his crown to Du Ling from the same clan, he practiced Daoism. According to legend, Du Yu turned into a cuckoo bird after his death—"Zigui" in the poem, with its legendary bloodcurdling cries to express his concern and care for the kingdom. Hence, Pi County was also called the "Cuckoo City" in ancient times. (By Guo Lili)

沃野蚕丛國

城荒杜宇基

井桥春酿雨

原柳晚垂丝

家解粉炊玉

人知竹酿醨

年～寒食節

清夜子規啼

衙道凝朝城

戴次壬寅芒種日

田翆書於成都

和青城题壁诗
hè qīng chéng tí bì shī

〔清〕骆成骧
qīng luò chéng xiāng

郁郁青城对赤城，深秋爽气扑人清。
yù yù qīng chéng duì chì chéng shēn qiū shuǎng qì pū rén qīng

书台草长重围合，仙洞花开四照明。
shū tái cǎo zhǎng chóng wéi hé xiān dòng huā kāi sì zhào míng

风过桂丛留客坐，雨余松盖倚天擎。
fēng guò guì cóng liú kè zuò yǔ yú sōng gài yǐ tiān qíng

玉真闲共金华语，子晋归来鹤夜声。
yù zhēn xián gòng jīn huá yǔ zǐ jìn guī lái hè yè shēng

Responding to the poem inscribed on the wall of Qingcheng Temple

Luo Chengxiang[1]
Qing Dynasty

Verdant Mount Qingcheng sits opposite of a crimson mountain,

the refreshing air of late fall soothingly invigorates.

Rambling grasses circle an ancient reading mound,

blooms surround a celestial cave radiant with color.

Travelers linger in breezes under fragrant osmanthus,

pine crowns rise straight and tall after the rains.

As Yuzhen and Jinhua idly chat,

Zijin descends with his calling crane in the night.

---

1   Luo Chengxiang (1865−1926), courtesy name Gongsu, was the top scholar in the imperial examination (Zhuangyuan)of Sichuan in the Qing Dynasty.In 1912, he served as the principal of Sichuan Higher School (the predecessor of Sichuan University), pioneering higher education.He also founded a secondary school in Chengdu, and engaged in education for a long time.

此诗由清代四川唯一的状元骆成骧所作，由赵熙书刻于青城山古常道观（今天师洞）壁，故称为"题壁诗"。青城山作为世界自然和文化双遗，素有"青城天下幽"的美名。诗人喜好游历，钟情山水，以细腻精微的笔触捕捉了青城山中花、草、林木等自然景观以及风、雨等气象变幻，呈现出青城山林木葱翠、诸峰环峙、丹梯千级、曲径通幽的自然之美。此外，青城山又属全真龙门派圣地，是中国四大道教名山之一，富有浓郁的道教文化历史和诸多传说故事。诗歌引经据典，以唐朝入道修仙的玉真公主和金华公主的闲话论道以及仙人王子晋骑鹤归来等典故，展现了青城山神秘丰厚的道教文化气息。

This poem was written by Luo Chengxiang, the top scholar in the imperial examination (Zhuangyuan) of Sichuan in the Qing Dynasty. The poem was later engraved by Zhao Xi on the wall of the ancient Daoist Temple (now Tian Shi Dong) on Mount Qingcheng. Hence, it is called "Poem on the Wall." As a world heritage site of both natural and cultural significance, Mount Qingcheng is known as "the most tranquil place on Earth." Luo Chengxiang was fond of traveling and loved mountains and waters. In delicate and subtle strokes, the piece depicts flowers, grass, trees and other natural scenes of Mount Qingchen as well as its unpredictable wind and rain. The poem unfurls the natural beauty of Mount Qingcheng with lush green forests, surrounding towering peaks, sky-high stone steps, and curving paths winding deep into seclusion. In addition, Mount Qingcheng is also a sacred place of the Quanzhen Sect of the Longmen School of Daoism, and one of the Four Great Daoist Mountains in China. Allusions to Princess Jinhua and Yuzhen's discussion of Daoism and the return of the immortal Wang Zijin riding a crane reference the mysterious and rich Daoist culture of Mount Qingcheng. (By Guo Lili)

攀：青城對赤
城深秋爽氣撲
人清書壹草長
重圓合儘洞花
開四照明風過
桂盖留宿坐雨
餘松盖倚天聲
玉真閑共金華
語子晉歸來鶴
夜聲
駱成驤　和青城縱望
歲次壬寅芒種
田旭中　書於成都